The Boss's Fake Fiance

Inara Scott

This book is a work of fiction. Names, characters, places, and incidents are the product of the author's imagination or are used fictitiously. Any resemblance to actual events, locales, or persons, living or dead, is coincidental.

Copyright © 2012 by Inara Scott. All rights reserved, including the right to reproduce, distribute, or transmit in any form or by any means. For information regarding subsidiary rights, please contact the Publisher.

Entangled Publishing, LLC
2614 South Timberline Road
Suite 109
Fort Collins, CO 80525
Visit our website at www.entangledpublishing.com.

Edited by Libby Murphy and Heather Howland
Cover design by Libby Murphy

ISBN   978-1-62266-851-9

Manufactured in the United States of America

First Edition October 2012

The author acknowledges the copyrighted or trademarked status and trademark owners of the following wordmarks mentioned in this work of fiction: Tiffany & Co., James Bond, Tesla Motors, Breakfast at Tiffany's, Twitter, BMW, Han Solo, Luke Skywalker, Chewbacca, Star Wars, Lord of the Rings, Louis Vuitton Cup, Klingon, Star Trek, Spock, Glenfiddich, Chanel.

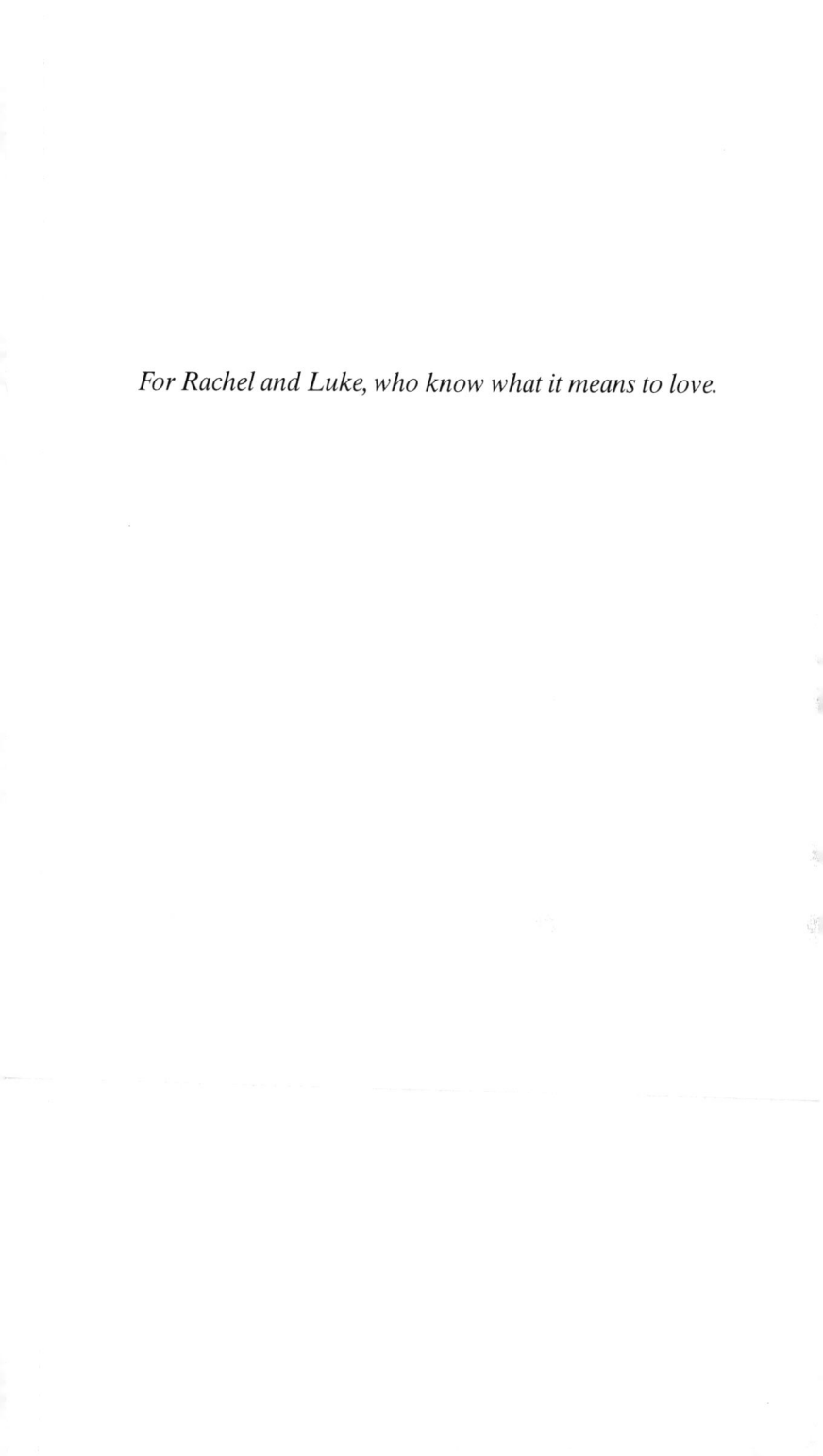

For Rachel and Luke, who know what it means to love.

Chapter One

Do not panic!

Melissa Bencher repeated the statement like a mantra, forcing the air in and out of her lungs. She plastered a smile on her face as her miserable, lying, cheating ex-boyfriend approached from across the crowded convention hall.

Do not hyperventilate. Do not faint. Do not vomit on his shoes.

On second thought, the last of those three didn't sound half bad.

Melissa tucked a stray piece of hair behind her ear. Waves of remembered humiliation washed over her as she thought about the last time she'd seen him, his pants around his ankles, screwing her best friend.

It wasn't your fault.

She wanted to believe this, but it was hard when she'd missed all the signs. The late nights at the lab. The secret emails. His new cologne. Things any other woman would have noticed, but she hadn't wanted to see.

She straightened her skirt, maintaining her smile through sheer force of will. She had known she might run into him here. The robotics and artificial intelligence community was actually rather small, and given that her new boss, Garth Solen, was there to give one of his rare keynote addresses, everyone who was anyone had come out to listen.

Melissa darted a look at the elegant, dark-suited figure sipping from a bottle of water in the AV area beside the stage. Garth was the founder of Solen Labs, a technology company that specialized in building advanced computing systems. Called one of the most brilliant businessmen and inventors of his time, he had built a technology empire in a little over a decade through sheer force of his will, creativity, and intelligence.

That's what the papers wrote about him. In person, of course, the first thing you noticed wasn't his mind: it was the sexy curve of his mouth, his broad, rangy shoulders, and thick black hair. Right now, he was clean shaven, but by the end of a long day he would have an astonishingly sexy five o'clock shadow that only seemed to accentuate his piercing gray eyes.

Not that she looked.

Okay, she looked. Some might say she had a crush. Melissa didn't think so, but if staring at someone's hands during meetings, finding herself occasionally unable to concentrate after a conversation in the hall, or memorizing the way he took his coffee was a crush, then fine, maybe she had one.

An AV tech stood next to him, showing him to how to adjust a headset. Garth didn't do podiums. It was remarkable he could work at a computer at all, given the amount of restless energy that constantly surged within him. In meetings, he'd spend half the time pacing around the room. He didn't slow down and didn't explain things twice.

It was like working for a tsunami.

Or a tornado.

Except way, way hotter.

Melissa hadn't expected *that* when she met him. She'd seen pictures, but they didn't do him justice. His mouth alone gave her goose bumps... Really, it wasn't fair that one man could combine sexy *and* smart in one six-foot package.

Not fair at all.

His only flaw—if one could call it that—was precisely the same thing that made him so intriguing. No one, it seemed, really knew Garth Solen. In the three months she'd worked for him, they'd seen each other almost every day, but she still couldn't get past his polished exterior. She knew his mind and the way he thought; he bounced ideas off of his employees constantly, challenged them to think beyond their assumptions, and never gave up when it came to making a product better. His ethics were absolute; he refused to take short cuts and was rigid about delivering quality.

But the person behind that? The human, vulnerable part of Garth Solen? He so rarely engaged in normal human rituals—small talk simply wasn't part of his vocabulary—she couldn't even guess what movies he liked, or which books lay beside his bed. He didn't do cocktail parties or social hours. When he came to conferences, he delivered his speeches, answered a few questions, and then left.

Mark stopped a few feet from her. "Melissa, is that you?"

She jerked her gaze away from Garth. Luckily, her unholy fascination with her boss had momentarily distracted her from Mark's approach, eliminating the need for a paper bag over her head.

"Mark?" She assumed a pleasant, nonchalant tone, though her insides shrank. "Fancy meeting you here."

He stopped a few feet away. Melissa forced herself to look straight into her ex-boyfriend's eyes for the first time in a year. Mark was five-seven, almost the same height as she was, but at thirty-eight—ten years her senior—he also had a touch of gray at the temples of his curly hair. He liked to call himself the absent-minded professor, but she knew he obsessed over his wardrobe, and never missed a date with his personal trainer.

She took in his appearance with a strangely clinical perspective. Was this really the man she'd dreamed about marrying? The one she'd moved across the country for? The one who'd broken her heart and left her in a dark, depressed state for months?

Hard to believe.

His eyes narrowed as they traveled from her high-heeled shoes to her long brown hair, with brand-new bangs and golden highlights. The hairdresser told her it made her blue eyes pop, and she hoped it was true.

"You look different." He said it with a hint of disapproval, or displeasure.

Melissa decided she liked the tone, either way. "Thanks." She made a point of running her fingers through her hair. "I'll take that as a compliment."

She knew she would never be a beauty queen—she was too thin, her chin too pointed, her eyes too big—but the experience of dealing with Mark's infidelity had changed her. It had been difficult to accept just how badly she'd been treated like a doormat, but once she had, she vowed to make some changes. The first had been her appearance. To her shock, she discovered that it felt better to wear a fitted pencil skirt and snug sweater than her usual outfit of oversized T-shirt and jeans.

When she'd been with Mark, she'd never had much interest in dressing up. She thought he loved her just the way she was—even if that wasn't particularly sexy or beautiful. Though secretly she'd always longed to know what it might feel like to have someone think she *was* beautiful, she told herself simply that wasn't what they had. They had something more, something different.

Or so she thought.

"Of course it is." He smiled gently, like a benevolent king. "How *are* you? Deanna and I...well, we worried about you. Leaving the way you did."

You mean, leaving because my best friend was screwing my BOYFRIEND? IN MY HOUSE?

Melissa longed to shout it out loud, but people were milling all around them, taking seats and preparing for Garth's address, and she refused to make a scene. "I'm fine."

"You've lost weight. Are you sure you're okay?"

The way he said it—the obvious pity and not a hint of guilt—sent a fresh surge of fury rushing through her. How dare he act like he'd done nothing wrong? Like he'd done her a favor by dating her at all? He'd said something in the moments that followed her discovery of him and Deanna that had lingered in her memory, and she heard it again now, echoing in her mind.

Melissa, I'm sorry, but men like me...well, we can't be expected to settle...

"I'm better than okay," she retorted, the remembered words rubbing like sandpaper against her skin. "I've got a new apartment and a great new job. I'm happier now than I've been in a long, long time."

Even as she said it, Melissa realized her words were actually true. Rebuilding a life wasn't easy and she'd put her family through hell along the way, but things *had* changed. She knew that every time she fell asleep thinking about a project from work, instead of imagining Mark and Deanna together. And every time she did her hair, or slipped on a new outfit, and didn't have to question whether it was worth it. Whether *she* was worth it.

"Working for *him*?" Mark indicated Garth incredulously. "You can't be serious. I've heard he's a nightmare."

"He's brilliant," she countered. "I've learned more in the last three months than I did in the past three years combined."

All of which were spent with you!

Mark frowned. "There's more to business than a big IQ, you know."

A tingle of interest pricked her spine at the petulant response. Was he jealous? Of Garth?

"Oh, it isn't just IQ," she replied airily. "He's got it all. Business savvy, an eye for design...it's no wonder he's been so successful."

She couldn't believe how enjoyable it was to watch the color leave Mark's face. Or see him clench his fists in anger.

"Come on," he scoffed. "I can't believe you've fallen for all that nonsense. He's got a great PR person, but is there really anything special underneath it all?" He made a sound of disgust. "I don't think so. He's nothing more than an outsized brain with a big ego."

Melissa fought the urge to punch her ex right in the middle of his supercilious face. A tiny voice in her head screamed to turn away and ignore him. But months of hurt and pain took over, and she couldn't seem to stop herself.

She leaned forward and touched his arm. "Sorry, but I have to be honest. Without a doubt, Garth Solen has most impressive...er...*mind*...that I've ever come across."

A thin line of white appeared around the corners of Mark's lips. Her immature revenge-seeking inner child danced with joy.

"Melissa," he said, voice strangled, "I hope you aren't suggesting that you've gotten mixed up with the man. You know what they call him, don't you? The human computer. He's got no emotions, 'Lis. I don't care how smart and rich he is. He's still a freak of nature."

Deliberately, she shrugged and gave a tiny, private smile. One that implied *she* knew the truth about such rumors. "If you say so."

Garth would kill her—absolutely massacre her—if he ever found out what she was insinuating. The truth was, even the people at Solen Labs who worked with him the most had little personal contact with him. The shield around his interior life was impenetrable. He didn't give out his phone number to anyone and never invited guests to his house. When he dated, the women were wealthy, gorgeous ice queens who exuded a chilly sophistication and *never* talked to the press.

But this wasn't about thinking, or planning. No, her head had stopped functioning a long time ago. She had given herself over to pure emotion.

"Never underestimate a computer," she added.

"He's just using you to get to me," Mark proclaimed, his voice gravelly with anger. "He's milking every bit of your experience in my lab so he can shut me down. Don't fool yourself. He'll drop you like a hot potato once he's gotten what he wants."

Melissa jammed her hands onto her hips. "How dare you," she said, low and furious. "You know nothing about it. Absolutely nothing."

"If you're so close to him, how come I haven't heard about it before now?" Mark leaned toward her, eyes narrow. "Is he ashamed of it? How long has this been going on, anyway?"

She stepped back, the intensity of his response bringing her down to earth with a thud. She mustn't start describing her imaginary relationship with Garth. If Garth found out she'd said something about him, she'd lose her job—and whatever respect he'd begun to feel for her—in a heartbeat.

Desperately, she sought a way out, short of admitting

she'd made the whole thing up. But she didn't actually *have* to explain anything, did she? She hadn't *said* they were dating. She'd suggested it, but she'd never actually *said* it, right?

She shot another quick look at Garth before turning back to Mark. "Believe what you want. I'm through with this conversation. I have no interest in seeing or talking to you ever again. Understand?"

He caught her arm. "Melissa, this is ridiculous. I don't want to fight. I came over here because I've been thinking that maybe I made a mistake. I wanted to say I was sorry."

"Sorry?" She drew back in disgust. "You think *maybe* you made a mistake? Are you kidding me?" She tried to pull her arm away, but he refused to let go. She straightened, rigid with anger.

"You should come back to California."

"Why? Because your lab is getting crushed by the competition?" She smiled with satisfaction. "You arranged the business so I had no control, remember, Mark? When I left, I didn't take anything with me other than my brain. Your lawyers couldn't do a thing about me working for Garth and I have no interest in getting back into business with you, especially not when your business is tanking."

Soon after she'd started working for Garth, Melissa had received a letter from Mark's attorneys requesting that she immediately cease and desist performing any work for Solen Labs. Her brother's fiancée, Tori, had quashed that effort with a few sharply worded letters of her own. Melissa hadn't violated any agreements or shared any confidential information. The law was clear: as long as Melissa was careful not to reveal any trade secrets, Mark was helpless to stop her.

"You vindictive little bitch." He bit out the words. "I told Deanna you weren't worth it."

Melissa stepped back, unprepared for the venom spewing

from him. She jerked her arm free. "You're disgusting. I've moved on, Mark. You should, too."

He called after her, but she turned on her heel and marched away, toward Garth and the soundstage.

She had the feeling she'd won, yet it didn't fill her with joy. Mark was pissed, and Melissa knew from experience that when pushed, he would do anything to strike back.

God help her if he succeeded.

Pulse racing, Melissa half-ran to the stage. Garth waved her over. He didn't smile—Garth guarded his smiles almost as closely as he guarded his email address—but he did give a worried frown when she reached his side.

"What was that all about?" he asked, looking back in the crowd.

"What?" She followed his gaze. It took a moment for her to realize what he was talking about. A flush of guilt warmed her cheeks, coupled with utter amazement that he'd noticed the dispute. "You mean Mark?"

Garth nodded. "Is he bothering you?"

Pleasure mixed with even more guilt. Was he *worried* about her?

"No."

"You're sure?"

He had a way of asking questions that demanded utter honesty. "Absolutely." She smiled, and even though Garth didn't return her smile, she thought she saw something soften in his eyes.

"Good." He straightened, and just like that, she knew the matter had been erased from his mind. "How's my tie?"

It was a tiny thing, but it was something a man would only ask a woman. And while she knew he saw her as nothing more than one of the many people who worked for him, the barest suggestion that he *did* see her as a woman—coupled with his concern that she was being bothered by Mark—sent a tingle straight through her body.

"May I?" She gestured toward his tie, and he nodded. She reached up to straighten it, and shivered when her hands touched the smooth cotton fibers of his shirt. The heat of his skin burned right through them and she quivered inside.

He's your boss! Stop it!

Melissa knew she was being silly. But her body didn't know that. And the warm rush of excitement that followed from the brief, almost imperceptible contact didn't know that, either.

As she adjusted a wrinkle from the knot, Melissa had the odd feeling that she was being watched. She shot a quick look over her shoulder to see Mark staring at her from across the room. With a fresh surge of pleasure, she left her hands on Garth's tie a fraction of a second longer than was necessary. Not long enough so that he'd notice, surely, but long enough so that Mark would.

"You're perfect." She forced an easy tone as she dropped her hands.

"Has anyone asked you about ThinkSpeak?"

ThinkSpeak was Garth's pet project—an artificial intelligence system that read and interpreted the brainwaves of children with severe autism, enabling parents and caretakers to understand their basic needs. Many doubted the technology—which was, admittedly, incredibly expensive—could ever be made commercial. Just last month, several members of the Solen Labs board of directors had suggested the company shelve the project indefinitely. In response, Garth had dumped millions of his personal funds into the development, but even his pockets weren't bottomless. He needed a big investor to sponsor continued development of ThinkSpeak, and he was determined to find one.

"I've had a few questions. I dodged them."

"Good. Until we hear back from Orelian, we need to keep things quiet."

Even before Melissa had started at Solen Labs, Garth had been courting one particular investor, Natalie Orelian, who expressed an interest in ThinkSpeak. Orelian was the only child of an old New York banking family. She had begun funding autism research when her grandson was diagnosed with a mild form of the disability at age three. While Orelian believed in funding new research, she shied away from projects that seemed too speculative or controversial. Garth was determined to keep any rumors about ThinkSpeak—good or bad—at bay until he had Orelian's support buttoned down.

A woman in a black shirt and pants approached them from the back of the stage. "They're ready for you, Mr. Solen."

"Right. Thanks, Melissa." Garth's intense gaze met hers for a moment before he turned away, and a delicious shiver passed up and down her spine. She glanced from his broad shoulders to the narrow line of his waist, perfectly displayed by his tailored suit. Her gaze followed him as he took the stairs in an easy bound.

But then, like a magnet, she found herself glancing at the back of the room, watching with a renewed feeling of dread as Mark caught her eye for one brief moment before he disappeared from the back of the room.

If Garth ever found out what she'd said…

Her stomach twisted in a painful knot of regret. She shouldn't have done it. Nothing justified her lies. Mark wasn't worth jeopardizing her job, or threatening the tiny, imperceptible chance that Garth might be developing some kind of interest in her.

Melissa turned back toward the stage and pushed the

dark thoughts from her mind. Garth would never find out what she'd said. And she would never make this mistake again.

...

Garth Solen pulled his silver Tesla Roadster parallel to the line of cars parked in front of a row of snug Brooklyn townhouses, and glanced at the woman sitting only a few inches away. He knew she'd stayed late to help him manage the crowds and steer away the more determined reporters, and he hadn't wanted her on the subway at night because of him. But now he was regretting the decision to give her a ride. The car had suddenly become a tiny, intimate space—a space he shouldn't be inhabiting with one of his employees.

"Thanks for bringing me home," Melissa said, shooting him a quick smile.

A fragrance moved across the dark interior as she bent forward to retrieve her purse. Something like flowers. Maybe roses. It was subtle and beautiful, like her.

Garth nearly choked on his own tongue as the thought slipped, unbidden, into his mind. "You're welcome," he managed to spit out. He jumped out of the car and walked around to open her door, forcing himself to take a slow breath as he did.

Forget it. She's off limits.

The truth was, Melissa Bencher had been getting under his skin for weeks. He found himself glancing at her in meetings far more often than he should, and then wondering if anyone had noticed. She had a creative, agile mind and a lovely smile—a little shy, like she wasn't sure how it would be received, yet infectious. And being with her tonight had been oddly…well…*comfortable*. Of course, they'd talked about work—challenges with a particular model, an issue with a patent—yet even that had been more relaxed somehow than he was used to.

But Melissa was in a class of women he absolutely refused to date. Employees, for one. Soft-hearted, for another. He preferred cold-hearted women. Women he knew weren't going to get messy and emotional. Life was simpler that way.

He tugged open the door, keeping his face carefully impartial. She stepped out of the car and he forced his eyes from her long legs to her piquant features. Too late, he realized that he'd blocked her from moving away from the car, and for a moment she stood just a few inches away, trapped beside him. The streetlight frosted her hair and illuminated a pair of full red lips.

"Did you—" Her voice trailed off as he stepped away quickly.

"Sorry," he said, clearing his throat. "What were you going to say?"

She adjusted her purse over her shoulder. "Nothing. Just good night. I'll see you tomorrow."

She hurried off toward her apartment. He watched as she unlocked the outer door and headed inside. Then he walked to the car and drove away without looking back.

Chapter Two

The next morning, Garth flicked the touch screen security lock on his tablet computer and then opened his email. He sipped his coffee as he scrolled through the messages, glancing every now and again through a large bay window as a show of pink and purple lit the morning sky. The fall colors of the maple trees surrounding the house sparkled and glowed as the sun hit the dew that had accumulated on their leaves.

He loved quiet mornings at his home in Scarsdale. The sprawling old Colonial mansion sat in the middle of ten wooded acres, about forty miles north of New York City. The house was close enough to commute to the Solen Labs office in Manhattan, but far enough away to avoid the traffic, tourists, and crowds of the city.

Garth had been accused of disliking people, but that wasn't true. He simply didn't trust them. He'd learned early in life that he was hardwired differently than most other people, and if there was one thing human beings didn't like, it was difference. People could be cruel, and that made it very difficult to want to strike up a relationship with them.

"Mr. Solen?" His housekeeper, Jessalyn Cislo, called

from the doorway. She had short black hair tipped with pink, a long string of earrings in one ear, and a colorful tattoo that curled from her wrist to her arm. His grandmother, who collected misfit people the way Garth collected hard drives, had suggested that he hire her a few years ago. He had been skeptical, but within a few minutes of meeting her, he'd been sold. Jessalyn was cynical, snarky, and the human equivalent of a lioness when it came to protecting him and privacy.

"Yes?"

"Nurse Simpson said your grandmother wanted to see you."

Garth's parents had died in a car accident when he was five, and he'd been raised by his grandmother, Patricia. Tender-hearted Nan had loved him like crazy, but she hadn't been much help to an awkward teenage boy trying to figure out how to navigate a world filled with bullies and girls who either laughed at him or looked right past him. It wasn't until college, when he'd grown into his tall frame and learned to mask his emotions, that he'd been able to make his way socially. But until then, Nan had provided the unconditional love he'd desperately needed, and he would lay down his own life to save hers.

At eighty-five, Nan still lived on her own, or at least she had until two weeks ago, when she developed a serious case of pneumonia. After spending a week in the hospital, she had begged to be allowed to go home. Reluctantly, Garth had spoken to her doctor, who had agreed to release her only after Garth had set up a virtual hospital room at his house, including round the clock care and a variety of machines to monitor every breath, heartbeat, and vital sign. The doctor said her condition was very serious, and she needed a lot of rest and quiet. While they had put her on a serious antibiotic, they couldn't be sure she would pull through.

Garth refused to consider that an option.

"Is everything all right?" he asked, a faint echo of nervousness curling in his stomach.

"I think so. She was smiling when I saw her." Jessalyn cocked her head at him. "Remember I'm leaving early today. Should I make something for you to heat up for dinner?"

Garth nodded. "Please. I have a conference call with Beijing at nine. I'll eat in my study."

"How about beef stroganoff and mashed potatoes?" She phrased it as a question, but it was really more of a statement. Or rather, a dare.

Garth winced. "Could you make a salad?" Jessalyn was obsessed with feeding him rich, heavy meals. Having Jess as a housekeeper was a little like having a second grandmother—in a pierced, tattooed body.

She crossed her arms over her chest. "I can make a Caesar."

Garth sighed. "Dressing on the side?"

Jessalyn sniffed loudly. "Fine. But I'm tossing in the bacon bits."

"Of course you are."

"Some reporters came to the gate last night," Jessalyn said. "I told them if they didn't get two hundred feet back, I would let out the dogs. And I'd bring my pepper spray. That seemed to convince them."

"Jess, you are a marvel," Garth said.

"Just earning my bonus."

He left Jessalyn and walked to the rear of the house, to a large bedroom suite he'd remodeled years before to accommodate a wheelchair, should his grandmother someday need it. So far, she didn't. Or hadn't. She'd been using one since she came home from the hospital, because the illness had left her so weak and unstable.

He knocked lightly on the door, and then headed in when he heard a chipper voice call out, "Come in!"

Looking more alert and energetic than she had for weeks, Garth's tiny, frail grandmother was sitting up in bed, cheeks rosy, a smile splitting her face. Her snowy-white hair was wrapped in bright blue curlers and covered with a lavender chiffon scarf. She clutched a newspaper in one hand.

"Is it true?" she demanded, as soon as he walked through the door. She clasped the paper to her chest and smiled even wider. "Oh, please tell me it's true!"

"What? Did they find the cure for cancer? Is Princess what's-her-name pregnant?"

She extended the paper toward him, tapping a picture. "No, no, don't be silly. Look for yourself. On page seventeen."

Garth raised a skeptical brow. "Is that the *New York Star Herald*? How many times have I told you to stop reading that tabloid, Nan? It doesn't actually contain news, you know. They make those stories up. Like the one about the aliens."

Nan pouted. "That could have happened. The government covers up all sorts of things."

"There are no aliens living in West Virginia."

"I hope not," she said fervently.

"And that time they said zombie elephants had been discovered at the Central Park Zoo?"

"Those creatures never move much," Nan said. "Haven't you always wondered about them?"

Garth masked a smile. Nan had always been gullible—it came with her trusting nature.

"I can't wait to see this," he said, taking the paper with a shake of his head.

As he focused on the picture, every muscle in his body tightened. The picture Nana had pointed to so eagerly was of him, opening the car door for Melissa the night before.

And the headline above screamed, "Garth Solen's Mystery Fiancée—Revealed!"

A wave of nausea passed over him. Quickly, he scanned the article. "Billionaire Garth Solen, notorious for discreet one-night stands and a stubborn refusal to settle down, is finally ready to take a bride. Sources close to the couple say new Solen Labs associate Melissa Bencher has stolen his heart, and the two are now engaged to wed..."

He looked up. "Nan, you don't—"

She interrupted him with a happy chirp. "Now, now, I know you didn't want me to find out this way. Really, dear, I know how private you are. You probably weren't quite ready to share the news with anyone, let alone the whole world at once. But it's out now, so you can tell me the truth." She held out a bony, arthritic hand, her fingers twisted with age, yet still surprisingly strong. He took her hand and sat down next to her bed. "It's a bit naughty of you to start a relationship with an employee," she continued, "but I understand. You must have a lot in common."

"Nan," he tried again. "Melissa and I, we aren't—"

"You aren't quite ready for marriage? Well, you're engaged now, dear. You'll have to get over that." She fixed him with an intense gaze. Her eyes—misty blue to his gray—began to sparkle with a hint of tears. "Garth, I know things haven't been easy for you. Girls can be terribly mean, and when that Samantha-hussy ran off with that necklace you gave her, well, my heart just broke."

Garth closed his eyes. "Not this again. That was years ago, Nan. Besides, the necklace was nothing special."

Nothing special.

That's what she said.

Garth laughed, humorlessly, to himself. How many times had he replayed Samantha's words? Her look of amusement when he'd given her the necklace, with its tiny diamond charm. Her response that she had no interest in getting serious. That she'd thought they were "nothing special." That she was dating other people, and he should, too. That maybe he shouldn't call her again, though she'd be glad to keep the diamond. It was pretty, after all.

Nan continued, unabated. "You can't be afraid. If you really love this girl, this Melissa, then you've got to take the leap. There are good women out there, and good people. You've got to let them in, or you'll always be alone."

This was a familiar argument, one he could respond to in his sleep.

"Nan, I wasn't meant for relationships. Women and I speak different languages. There's really no point in trying."

"I'm not saying it will be easy. It wasn't easy for your grandfather, either, but he found me, didn't he?" Nan smiled at the memory.

Garth rolled his eyes. "Yes, he did. But we can't all be so lucky. Besides, I'm not alone," he added, as he always did. "I've got you, and Solen Labs, and—"

"Solen Labs isn't a person," she interrupted, in a surprisingly fierce voice. "And I'm not always going to be here."

He paused. She'd given her standard response, but somehow it felt different when she was lying in a bed, surrounded by blinking machines, with a nurse on standby. "Don't say that."

Nan gripped his hand tightly. "Life is meant for love, dear, not solitude."

Garth forced a laugh. "I'm the human computer, remember? I'm doing just fine."

She waved a hand. "That's nonsense. They don't know you." She paused to cough, and the deep, rattling sound made

Garth's stomach twist. When the fit had passed, she leaned back against the pillows, her face white and drawn. "You're more than what they see."

He tried one more time. "I was just dropping Melissa off after the conference," he said. "I can't imagine why they followed us home."

Nan's eyes popped open and she sucked in a breath. "Oh! I hadn't even thought about that." She tapped the newspaper. "There must be a leak. The article says 'sources close to the couple.' They can't make that up, you know. There must have been someone who told them the news. You should get Jessalyn to hunt down the culprit. She's very good at that. I suspect she could have been a detective."

Garth ran his fingers through his hair. Why did he always seem to lose control of the conversation when he was with Nan? Next thing he knew, she would be sending Jessalyn into Solen Labs to track down a Russian spy. Or an alien. Or a zombie elephant.

"When can I meet her?" Nan asked. "I don't mean to sound like a silly old lady, but I can't tell you how much easier I'll sleep, knowing that you've finally found a match."

The absolute conviction in her voice chilled him. What the hell was he supposed to do now? Insist that there was nothing between him and Melissa? Demand that she listen to him, when she was so convinced that the story was true? And so damned happy about it?

"Nan," he started again. "Nan, there's been a mistake. You see, Melissa and I are friends."

She giggled, a tiny, happy sound. "That's wonderful, dear. The best matches always start out that way. But I can see it in her eyes. She's terribly in love with you."

Garth focused on the soft, fragile hand he held inside his own. He pictured Dr. Caldy, telling him to keep Nan quiet and rested, explaining that elderly people with pneumonia often became fatigued and confused, and required extra care, rest, and an absence of stress.

Which meant one thing: he couldn't tell her the truth.

She was still so fragile, barely sleeping at night because of the violent coughing. Her body, with a weak heart and an aging set of lungs, was struggling to recover from the ravage of the disease. This story gave her peace, without which she'd never heal.

"I don't know," he hedged. "Maybe once you're recovered."

Nan sat up a few inches. She shook her head sadly. "Garth, dear, you have to be realistic. I may not recover from this."

He snorted, even as a deep, sick feeling twisted his gut. "Now you're talking nonsense."

"I'm eighty-five. You know the odds."

"Don't talk to me about odds, Nan." He stood and paced to the window, staring at the lush green lawn beyond. "You've beaten every odd you've ever been given. You will recover. Look how much better you're feeling already."

"Garth!" Her voice took on the stern quality that had always brought him round as a boy. He turned and slowly met her gaze. "Garth, no more pretending. No more kidding around. I've got a bad heart and a case of pneumonia. If this cough doesn't kill me, my ticker will. I've been holding on because I know you need me, but I can't do it forever. I need the rest, and I can't get it as long as I'm sitting up at night wondering what will happen to you after I die."

Garth felt the blood drain from his face. "Nan," he said, "is that how you've been feeling lately? Like you can't rest because of me?"

She set her jaw in an expression he knew from his childhood. "No pity from you, young man. I'm just saying I want to meet this girl while I still have the chance."

He paused, his thoughts spinning. How in the world could he pull this off? "She's had a cold, Nan. Maybe it isn't a good idea."

"I need to meet her."

The underlying pain in her voice was his undoing. He would make this work. He *had* to make it work.

"I'll do my best," he said, his eyes flicking to the machines beside her bed. "Maybe this weekend."

"Thank you, dear. Now, I probably ought to take a nap. I want to be at my best when I meet your bride-to-be." Nan sighed with obvious relief and closed her eyes.

Garth rose, filled with equal parts dread, pain, and frustration. He had no idea how to extricate himself from this situation without sending Nan into a tailspin, which meant that he would have to play along with her for a little while. At least until she was out of the woods, and the pneumonia had passed.

Meanwhile, whatever fool had made up this story would suffer. He would see to it personally.

Chapter Three

Melissa's computer dinged to notify her of an incoming email. She ignored it, staring at the piece of rebellious computer code on her screen. She'd been wrestling with the language for over an hour this morning, and she'd been able to tune out her demanding inbox for most of that time. She loved pouring all of her attention into a problem, knowing the satisfaction that would come with success. At times like this, she felt overwhelmed with gratitude that Garth had given her a chance. She'd always loved her work, but she loved it even more now that she was doing it on her own, without Mark breathing over her shoulder. If only she could focus long enough to…

Ding.

Ding.

Ding.

Melissa turned off the volume on her computer, but the incoming messages kept flashing on the bottom of her screen.

Another.

And another.

With a growl of irritation, Melissa clicked open her inbox.

And blinked. Sixty messages? In one hour? The most recent was from her brother, Ross. She could practically hear his voice in the regarding line: "Open your damn email and call me!"

She paused for a moment when she saw the email, with a single link illuminated. Virus? No, Ross had included one other line of text: "'Lis, what the hell is going on?"

Suddenly nervous, she clicked on the link. A pause. Spinning circle in her web browser. A grainy image slowly filled the screen, beneath a screaming black headline.

She froze, scalp tingling.

No, no, no, no, no...

But there she was, holding Garth's hand as he helped her from the passenger seat of his Tesla. His face was hard to make out—the photographer must have been at an awkward angle—but her face, and the goofy smile on her lips, was painfully clear.

"Engaged?" she whispered in horror. "Ready to tie the knot?"

The photographer must have been hiding in a doorway a few doors down from her townhouse, or maybe even lounging by a streetlight, camera hidden somewhere in the fold of a long coat. She would never have noticed him. Even if she had, she never would have thought he might be waiting to take a picture. A picture that would appear on the cover of a tabloid, viewed by millions of readers.

Only one word described this situation: *disaster*. Complete and total disaster.

She dropped her head into her hands.

She was going to jump off the Verrazano Bridge.

No—she was going to find Mark, hit him over the head with something very heavy, and then drag *his* body over the side of the bridge with her when she jumped.

Because Mark was the only possible explanation for the picture and the story. She'd never said a word about dating Garth to anyone else. Mark must have gone straight out of the convention hall and told a reporter they were getting engaged. Planted the story so Garth would publicly announce that they weren't dating.

All to humiliate her one more time.

She dug her phone out of her purse, hands shaking. She'd turned off the ringer for Garth's speech yesterday and had evidently forgotten to turn it back on.

Fifteen missed calls. Seven from unknown numbers, four from her mother, two from Ross, one from her brother Joe, and one from Tori. She listened to Tori's message first, cringing when she heard the amused but concerned voice. "This is a joke, right? Call me right away when you get this. If Brit finds out, he'll flip."

Unable to contemplate speaking to Tori right at that moment—let alone her overprotective older brother—Melissa texted a quick message instead.

Tabloids are crazy!! Nothing going on with Garth! LOL!

If only she could be as nonchalant as her text.

"I take it you've seen the picture?"

Melissa jerked upright and choked when she heard his voice at the door of her office. He loomed there, looking like the grim reaper, come to take her with him to hell. "Garth!"

His jaw was a rigid line, his steely gray eyes dark, his brows drawn together. He wore his usual workday garb—blue oxford, top button open, fitted black trousers. She found herself staring at the lean cast of his hips for a long moment before jerking her eyes back to his scowling face.

Bad idea to stare at the man's pants when you're about to lose your job, 'Lis.

"May I?" He started to close the door to the office.

She nodded unsteadily, heart racing, and then got to her feet so her eyes weren't positioned exactly at his groin. The door clicked shut, and the room suddenly seemed ten times smaller. Melissa's office was the end of the hall, a light, open space with a tinted-glass window looking out onto 32nd Street. But right now it felt like a tiny, dark bubble.

Garth, of course, did not sit.

"The picture," he prompted. "You've seen it, I assume?"

Melissa nodded miserably. "Just now." She indicated the phone in her hand. "Apparently my mother has, too. And my brother. And my other brother. And Tori, and then—"

He cut her off with a raised hand. "Please. I get it. Everyone in the tri-state area has seen the damn thing."

"Actually, Tori called from Scotland, so it's way beyond a tri-state sort of thing," Melissa replied. She instantly wished she could withdraw her words, as Garth pushed his thumbs into his temples and blew out a loud breath.

"Again, thanks," he bit out.

"Sorry." She lowered herself back into her seat.

End of job. End of career. End of whatever fantasy she'd begun to develop about Garth having feelings for her.

"What did you tell them?"

"I haven't had a chance to call them back yet. They left messages while I was on the subway to work."

"Good," she thought she heard him say under his breath. But that was absurd. Why would he care what she told her parents?

Melissa drew in a deep breath. She had to tell him what she'd done. She had to. Even if it meant her job. If she didn't come clean, her conscience would eat away at her soul.

Yet the words didn't come. Her mouth flopped open and then closed, like a fish.

"This whole thing is a nightmare," he said, as he began

to pace back and forth. "If I get my hands on that Stanley Hartwaddle—"

"Stanley who?" Melissa asked.

Garth waved a hand. "You know, the reporter. Stanley Hartwaddle. The one who published that ridiculous thing. I still can't believe people are actually falling for it. I swear, I got at least ten calls on my way to the office, and those are the people who should know better."

Melissa frowned. "It's not *that* ridiculous," she said. A tiny bit of her guilt was replaced with annoyance at his dismissive tone.

"Of course it is," Garth snapped. "Engaged? Me and you?"

A little more of the guilt slipped away. "What are you trying to say? It's not like I'm some kind of monster, you know." Melissa fluffed her bangs and sniffed. "These things do happen."

Garth stared. "You're not going to get all sensitive on me, are you? That's the last thing I need."

"Sensitive? I'm being *sensitive*?" Annoyance bubbled over into irritation.

"Melissa..." He spoke slowly and calmly. "All I said was that people should know better than to think I'd be dating someone like you."

"Someone like me?" she squeaked, eyes popping wide. "What the hell is that supposed to mean?"

Garth pressed a hand over his eyes. "I didn't mean anything wrong by that. I'm just saying that I usually date women a little, well, *tougher*. You're too nice."

Melissa crossed her arms over her chest. "That's the worst attempt at a compliment I've ever heard."

"What are you talking about?"

"I'm not some kind of namby-pamby nice girl," she said.

"I happen to be extremely tough."

"You're offended that I said you're nice?" Garth's scowl blackened.

"You've got to admit that it's not entirely crazy that people would believe something like this," Melissa threw back. At some point during this conversation she had lost her fear of Garth, and was now simply furious with him for being so dismissive. "After all, we do work closely together. And it isn't as though there are a lot of women around the office. When you think about it, it's perfectly natural that someone might dream up a story like this."

"It's like talking to Nan," Garth muttered to himself, eyes raised toward the ceiling. He blew out a breath. "Let's rewind, okay? We've got a situation here and I don't really care how plausible it is or isn't. Someone told a reporter we're getting engaged. Apparently, everyone in the free world has already heard the story, and it's only—" he made a point of checking his watch— "nine-thirty in the morning." He resumed pacing.

Melissa nibbled on the end of one fingernail, her bluster seeping away as she recalled exactly *how* the rumor had likely begun. "You've probably dealt with this sort of thing before, right? I assume if we just ignore it, in a few days the story will disappear completely."

And if it does, you'll never need to know who started it in the first place.

"Well, actually, that's what I need to talk to you about." Garth stopped pacing long enough to bury his hands in his pockets. His eyes slid away from hers, looking vaguely uncomfortable. "We might need to…ah…play along for a little while."

"Play along?" Melissa repeated. "What do you mean?"

Garth dropped into the chair beside the desk. He paused, as if collecting his thoughts. "What if I told you I had a reason why I needed to keep the story going, just for a few weeks?"

Melissa laughed. "I'd say you were crazy."

He stared at his hand, clenching and unclenching his fist. "Great. So after that, what would you say?"

"You're kidding, right?" Melissa stared, unable to believe what she was hearing.

"No. I'm not."

"Garth, we can't pretend to be engaged. That's, that's..." she sputtered, unable to complete the thought.

"Crazy, yeah, I got that. But it doesn't have to be that big a deal. We play along with the press for a couple of weeks, and then we get unengaged." He shrugged, spreading his hands to indicate how incredibly unimportant the prospect of getting married was. "Simple."

Melissa gave a short laugh, hardly believing his nonchalance. "Garth, most people make a *very* big deal out of getting engaged. They make announcements. They tell their friends. They get engagement rings, and have parties and tell their parents."

"I'm not most people," he noted.

"Well, that's clear," Melissa said. "Why in the world would you want to do this? You hate publicity. I assumed you were furious about the story."

"I was. And am. Whoever planted that story is going to pay, believe me." He paced the room, flexing his hands in frustration. "You don't have any idea who might have said something, do you? Usually, these things start somewhere."

Melissa shivered. She had hoped that they might be able to ignore the whole thing, and her involvement would never have to come to light. But evidently, Garth was not going to let this story fade away without finding out the truth. And as terrified as she was to tell him the truth, the prospect of hiding it and having him find out later was far worse.

"Actually, I think I might," she forced herself to say.

He straightened. "Really?"

"Yes." Feeling like she was plunging into a deep abyss, Melissa continued. "It was me."

...

Garth froze. It took approximately twenty seconds for the surge of anger to travel from his gut to his brain. And then explode from his lips. "You? *You* planted the story? *You* told Stanley we were getting engaged?"

"No, no, no!" Melissa said quickly. "I never talked to any reporter."

"Explain," he bit out.

How had he missed the signs? Why had he trusted her, even for a minute?

Melissa swallowed twice, in rapid succession. "You remember how I was talking to Mark Venshiner at the conference yesterday? Well, the thing is, he and I were pretty serious for a while."

"You were involved with Venshiner?" Garth's lip curled. He'd known Melissa had worked for Venshiner, thanks to the cease and desist letters that Mark's attorney had sent to try to keep Melissa from working for Solen Labs. Still, he hadn't realized the two had been romantically connected.

Garth had only met Mark in person a few times. He'd been left with the general impression of an arrogant blowhard who thought far more of himself than his intelligence and skills deserved.

An image of Venshiner grabbing Melissa's arm the day before appeared in Garth's mind, and he felt a surge of protective anger. Venshiner had a reputation as an academic who liked his graduate students young, pretty, and naïve.

Garth hadn't liked the man before. He liked him even less now.

"Yes." Melissa paused. "It didn't end well."

"So you told him we were getting engaged? Because you had a thing that ended badly?"

"No, no, it wasn't like that." She shook her head, and a few strands of long dark hair, highlighted with flashes of golden honey, escaped from the loose knot on top of her head. She tucked them behind her ears. He couldn't help but notice her hands were shaking.

Garth tried to shake a surge of defensiveness at the obvious tremor of fear. He wasn't the one who caused this mess—she was. So why did he have the sudden urge to apologize? To tell her everything would be all right?

"I just, sort of, well, *implied* that we were seeing each other," Melissa said. "I never said we were engaged."

"Then where did the story come from?" He kept his voice even. Calm.

Melissa got up from her desk to peer out of her window. The narrow line of her body looked vulnerable, silhouetted by soft morning light. "I don't know for sure." Her voice shook, and she cleared her throat. "When he left me yesterday, Mark was pissed. Really pissed. I was trying to make him jealous, and I think it worked. I shouldn't have done it, I know that. But I had no idea he'd take it this far."

"You think he called a reporter and made up this whole story because he was jealous?" Garth stared in astonishment. "That's absurd. Who would do such a thing?"

"Mark," she said, still looking out the window.

Garth narrowed his eyes. "Are you sure *you* weren't the one who talked to the reporter? If you were trying to make Venshiner jealous, this would have been right up your alley."

Melissa spun around, her mouth falling open in surprise.

"You think *I* planted the story? That's crazy. Besides, if I'd done something that dumb, I obviously wouldn't have told you about it."

Garth shrugged. "Forgive me, but nothing about your story is particularly rational."

He regretted the words the minute he saw Melissa's back snap straight, and her face flush. Damn it, how could the simplest observation make women so emotional?

"The guy cheated on me, okay? I was hurt and embarrassed. I wanted a little revenge. Haven't you ever done anything crazy because you were hurt?"

His gaze flickered to the full lower lip that she'd caught between her teeth. Something about the curve of that lip made it hard to maintain his anger. "I still don't understand why he would have said anything to a reporter," he said, forcing his gaze back to her bright blue, pleading eyes.

"Mark knows how private you are," she said. "He must have figured if he spread a story like this, it would piss you off, and you'd make some public statement about how we aren't together. He wanted to humiliate me, and he figured this was the best way to do it."

Garth pictured Nan's eager face when she held out the paper. He gritted his teeth at the renewed flare of anger. "Did you have any idea how much trouble you could cause? Didn't you think for a minute about who might be affected by this?"

"I thought it was a harmless story." Melissa spoke through clenched teeth. "I'm sorry for causing problems for you, but it's not like this isn't causing problems for me, too. I have no doubt my mother is flipping out right now, my brothers are probably ready to string me up for hiding this from them, and it will take me a week to respond to all these emails." She gestured toward her computer, which had been steadily pinging with the arrivals of new messages.

Garth crossed his arms over his chest. "So sorry for your email troubles, but my grandmother caught sight of that picture. She's absolutely convinced we're getting married."

"So?" Melissa shook her head. "Surely she knows you well enough to know it's just a story."

"Nan tends to believe the things she reads in the paper."

"That's why you want to pretend we're engaged?" Her brows knit together in a confused line. "Because your grandmother believes it?"

"I tried to explain the truth this morning and she refused to listen. Once she gets something in her head, it can be impossible to shake."

Garth couldn't believe he was actually explaining himself to her. Yet, as furious as he was with her for what she'd done, he had to admit he needed her help. He could hardly pull off a fake engagement on his own.

"So you need me to marry you because your grandmother read in a tabloid that we were engaged." Melissa blinked. "You're joking. You've got to be joking."

"Nan's recovering from pneumonia." The words were an effort. He hated that he had to reveal so much. "She's also got a bad heart. She's incredibly weak and needs to rest and recover without any stress. She worries about me being alone, and thinking I was engaged gave her a moment of peace."

"I'm really sorry about your grandmother," Melissa said, "but surely you can't think I'd marry you simply because she's sick."

Garth tried not to imagine the joy on Nan's face when he entered the room that morning, or the pain she'd feel if he tried to tell her the truth. His voice felt like it was coming from far away. He didn't want to beg—he *wouldn't* beg—but he needed Melissa's help. "We wouldn't really get married— we'd just pretend for a few weeks, until she's recovered enough to hear the truth. She started on antibiotics last week, and her doctor said if all goes well, she'll be able to start getting up and about by the end of the month. Then we can break it off and go on with our lives."

"The end of the month." Melissa paused and pursed her lips, as if consulting some mental calendar. "And today's October 11. So in three weeks we just break it off? How would I explain it to my friends, my family…?" She spread her hands in bewilderment.

"You'll have to figure that out," he said tightly. "You made this mess, Melissa, and now you're going to fix it."

"I said I was sorry!"

"Great. You're sorry." He nodded in acceptance. "Consider this one big apology." He pulled open the door of her office, hoping like hell that he had correctly interpreted her look of defeat. "Now, cancel any appointments you have for the rest of the day and meet me in the lobby in fifteen minutes. We're going to get a ring."

Chapter Four

Over the next fifteen minutes, Melissa ignored ten more phone calls, canceled four meetings, sent quick text messages to her mother and brothers Ross and Joe, and then turned off her cell phone so she didn't have to see their responses. With a mountain of email still staring at her, she shut down her computer and slipped on her cherry-red trench coat. The deliberately cheerful garment had little impact on her bleak, overwhelmed mood. She met Garth in the Solen Labs reception area, and then followed him to the parking garage located under the building.

"What did you tell your family?" Garth asked

"I said things were moving fast and I'd call later tonight." Was she really doing this? It all felt so impossibly unreal. She wasn't even sure she had a real choice in the matter. She was acutely aware that Garth held all the cards in their relationship, and if he wanted to force her to participate in this game, he could.

"Our arrangement will have to be kept a secret. From everyone."

Her chin jutted out stubbornly. "I'm not going to lie to

my parents."

"Then don't talk to them at all. But I won't have you telling them the truth. The more people that know, the more chance of something going wrong."

"Like what?" she cried. "What *else* could possibly go wrong?"

"How about an even bigger headline?" he said. "Like 'Garth Solen's *Fake* Fiancée.' Forgive me if I'd rather not see *that* on the front page of the *New York Star Herald*. Nan isn't the only one who would freak out, you know. I've got Natalie Orelian to worry about, too."

"The ThinkSpeak investor? Why are you worried about her?"

"The woman is obsessed with protecting her family name. If she hears a hint of scandal—about the product or about Solen Labs—she'll disappear. I know she will. But once I get her to sign the investment agreement, it doesn't matter."

Melissa paused. Only Garth Solen could make an utterly ridiculous plan sound logical and rational. "We've only known each other for three months," she said. "No one will believe we're really engaged."

"You were just telling me how believable it is," he pointed out.

"I'm terrible at lying," she warned.

He surveyed her with an impassive gaze. "Right."

Melissa's mouth dropped open. "Now that's uncalled for!"

"Uncalled for?" He frowned. "First of all, *I* didn't even say anything—"

"I can tell what you're thinking," she interrupted.

"Second of all," Garth continued, "I'm not the one who made up a story about us dating and spread it to her vindictive ex-boyfriend!"

"Yes, and we've established that was *dumb*," she grumbled. "That doesn't give you the right to be mean."

"I'm being mean?" He gestured in frustration. "How in the world did this become *my* fault?"

"What about afterward?" she pressed. "Three weeks from now, you dump me *and* fire me? Oddly enough, that doesn't sound too appealing."

Garth made a sound, low and garbled, in the back of his throat. "So you can dump me. I don't care."

"And my job?"

He paused. "At the risk of insulting you *again*, I'm not sure it's a good idea for you to keep working for me after this is over. People won't understand. It will seem…odd."

With that simple, rational statement, a piece of Melissa's heart shattered. She loved her job at Solen Labs. Every day she came to work, she discovered some new challenge. Her brain was alive here as it had never been before, and the thought of losing her work was devastating.

But she had to admit Garth had every right to ask her to leave. She'd lied about him and created a terrible situation as a result. She deserved to lose her job.

Something of her heartbreak must have shown in her face, because Garth sighed. "Why don't we play it by ear? Maybe the fuss will die down more quickly then I imagine. If not, I know some other people working on projects like yours. I'll help you find something new."

Melissa nodded. "Thanks," she said, defeated.

It wasn't perfect, but it was better than nothing.

"Will you get in the car now?"

She nodded, and Garth unlocked the door. For a moment, she was transported back to the night before. The surprise comfort and ease she'd felt in his presence. The rapport they'd established talking about work. The passion in his voice when he'd talked about ThinkSpeak.

Of course, any supposed closeness was gone now. Melissa got into the car and Garth roared out of the parking garage with a squeal of tires. As soon as they were out on the highway, he pulled out his phone.

"I need to talk to Tori." His voice could have split a glacier.

Tori must have been waiting beside the phone, because Garth started talking almost immediately. He explained in a few, terse statements what had occurred, from Melissa's theory that Mark had planted the story, to his own concern for his grandmother. After making the entire fake engagement sound utterly and completely reasonable, Garth handed the phone to Melissa. "She wants to talk to you," he said.

The quiet electric engine of Garth's Telsa did little to cut the silence that hung over the small space. She took the phone awkwardly, making sure not to touch his fingers.

"Hi, Tori," Melissa said cautiously. She almost dropped the phone when the other woman's voice jumped out through the receiver.

"Geez, Melissa, you're still alive, right? Any bleeding? Visible wounds?"

Melissa hid a smile. Tori tended to be a bit dramatic. "Of course I'm alive. I just texted you an hour ago."

"Yeah, but now Garth has you stuffed in his car. I can't believe he hasn't killed you."

Melissa darted a quick look at the steely-jawed man beside her. Her heart skipped a beat. It was like riding in the car with freaking James Bond—his dark gaze intent, collar unbuttoned, one hand resting confidently on the steering wheel as he darted in and out of traffic like they were being pursued by a pack of Russian bad guys. A bright electronic control panel illuminated the middle of the dashboard, depicting a street map along with a variety of statistics about the car's performance, and she imagined it having a secret button that would turn the car into a plane, or high-speed motorboat.

Thinking of James Bond made her think of her eldest brother, and her stomach twisted. "Is Brit there?" she asked Tori, ignoring the comment about Garth.

"No. He's out hiking up a mountain with some guys he met in a pub last week. I swear, he's trying to go local, Melissa. He's even growing a beard!"

Melissa paused to try to take in the image of her exquisitely groomed brother growing a beard. She shook her head. "You've got to be kidding me. My brother? Growing a beard?"

When Melissa was a freshman in college, Brit had taken over as CEO of Excorp, the family business. Over the next ten years, he'd turned around the small, failing business, eventually taking it public for millions of dollars. Along the way, he'd played the part to the hilt, working eighty-hour weeks, dating a series of supermodels, and living in an incredible penthouse apartment in Manhattan. It wasn't until he'd met and fallen in love with Tori that he'd realized he had lost himself somewhere along the way. Three months ago, he'd taken an indefinite leave of absence from the business to fulfill a lifelong dream to travel to Scotland. Melissa was thrilled that he was finally taking time to do what he wanted, and even more thrilled that he'd finally stopped playing overprotective father to her and her other two brothers.

Tori giggled. "I think he's developing an accent, too. It's hilarious. I'm going to have to start calling him Scot instead of Brit."

"As long as he's not bothering me," Melissa said, "more power to him."

It wasn't that Melissa didn't have a father. She did. And

a mother, too. But her parents had never been particularly... well...*parental*. Brit had always been the one Melissa turned to for advice and support, and part of her longed to do that now. But even as she imagined him swooping in to protect her and fix her mistakes, as he always had in the past, another part of her knew she needed to handle this on her own. Brit had driven her crazy trying to "fix" her depression, and his meddling had almost cost him the love he now shared with Tori. They both needed a little distance, and this time, Melissa was determined not to let him get involved.

"Are you going to tell him?" she asked Tori, dreading the response.

"You mean, am I going to tell him that Garth is strong-arming you into playing his fake fiancée?"

Melissa closed her eyes. "Um, yeah."

"Not bloody likely," Tori said cheerfully. "He'd probably cut the trip short just to throttle you *and* Garth. He's starting to get over his father-complex, but I suspect that might just push him back over the edge."

"So what are you going to say?" Melissa asked.

"Hopefully, nothing," Tori replied. "The papers here don't really give a rip about it. I only know because I have an alert that notifies me if anything pops up about Garth on the Internet. As Garth's lawyer, I don't like surprises. Frankly, neither does he."

"So I gathered," Melissa said dryly.

"He's pretty pissed?"

"You think?"

"Well, don't tell him I said this, but I completely understand why you did it. People do crazy things when they're hurt."

Melissa blinked away a sudden tear. She couldn't talk to Tori about Mark. Not now. Not in front of Garth. "Look, I better go. Let me know if Brit hears anything, okay?"

"Got it. You take care of yourself. And don't think too badly of Garth. He comes off a bit brusque, but there's a sweet guy underneath it all."

Sweet? Melissa could think of a lot of adjectives to use at that moment to describe Garth Solen, but none of them were anything like "sweet."

Chapter Five

For the next ten minutes, Garth wove through thick traffic, a ticking muscle in his jaw betraying his frustration. Melissa winced at every abrupt stop and start. Garth's refusal to give her even the tiniest bit of understanding had done wonders to eliminate her lingering feelings of guilt, but nothing could eliminate the knot of anxiety in the pit of her stomach.

They finally pulled up in front of a tall, marble-clad building on Sixth Avenue. A man wearing a black cap and dark suit waiting on the curb ran around to the driver's side.

"Mr. Solen?" he asked.

Garth put the car into park. "Yes. We won't be long."

He left the car running as he jumped out. Cabs piled up behind them, honking their horns. Melissa looked everywhere but at Garth as he extended a hand to help her from the car. She ignored him and got out as quickly as she could and started walking. Seemingly unperturbed by her obvious attempts to pretend he was not there, Garth's long legs made short work of the distance between them. With a casual but deliberate move, he reached out and touched the small of her back, guiding her toward the building ahead. She tensed, not wanting to feel her body react to him. But it did, and she found herself leaning against his hand, unwillingly relishing the gentle pressure of his touch.

"I don't know if there will be press here," Garth said, his mouth barely moving, "but you should know there's bound to be talk about our visit."

Melissa finally paused and looked at their destination. "Garth, why the hell did you bring me to Hadrien? Are you *trying* to whip the press into a frenzy?"

Hadrien was an exclusive jewelry store known for catering to only the wealthiest clients. Rumors had it that the manager checked the portfolio of anyone who wanted to walk through the exclusive steel doors. Their signature engagement rings—set with enormous four and five-carat rose-hued diamonds—were a New York tradition.

"My grandmother loves it here. She'll expect it. Now try to act engaged. I want this to look real."

The pressure on her back did not change, and Garth did not look at her as they moved toward the building. Melissa gritted her teeth. Clearly, he wasn't interested in her idea of "real." That would have involved sweet nothings, loving glances, and maybe, *possibly*, something like a smile.

They were greeted at the door by a man wearing a pinstriped navy suit. He was tall, with a massive chest, dark skin, and close-cropped white hair. "Welcome to Hadrien," he said, a majestic lilt in his deep voice. "And congratulations." He extended a hard to Melissa and dropped her a tiny wink. "I'm Tennyson Merrysman, but you can call me Ten."

She shook hands nervously, feeling impossibly small and gauche as her unpolished nails disappeared into his massive palm. "Nice to meet you."

He gave her hand a gentle squeeze before extending his hand to Garth. "Mr. Solen, sir. Good to see you again. I appreciate you thinking of us for this important occasion."

"Of course. Thanks for seeing us on short notice, Ten."

Ten pulled open the door and gestured for them to walk inside. "Shall we?"

As if he'd heard her earlier thoughts, Garth paused, looked down at her, and pulled her closer to his side. His hand closed around her waist as the ghost of a smile touched his lips. "I can't wait."

Their hips brushed together. The feeling of his body, pressed against hers, sent a shiver along Melissa's spine.

Breathe. In and out. Breathe.

They walked through the doorway. Garth's fingers splayed out along her curve of her hip and Melissa wobbled on her heels. The tiny, deliberate smile on his lips turned into something more annoying. Something deliberate. Pleased.

Melissa considered smacking him.

That wouldn't look real, now, would it?

"Ms. Bencher?"

Melissa heard Ten's voice as if from a distance. She realized he must have said something to her, but she had no idea what it was. "What?" She cleared her throat. "I'm sorry, what did you say?" She tried to speak normally, but her voice cracked.

"She's a little overwhelmed," Garth said to Ten.

Melissa bristled at the condescending tone but forced herself to laugh.

Ten smiled encouragingly. Melissa had the feeling he'd dealt with more than a few overwhelmed brides. "Don't worry," he promised. "We'll take care of you."

As they walked, Garth and Ten talked about a necklace Garth was having made for Nan for Christmas. Melissa tried not to gape at the dark-hued elegance of the store. This was a far cry from the hustle and bustle of Tiffany's, or some of the other jewelry stores she'd visited with her mother over the years. There was just one long glass case against the wall, with security guards at either end, a tall, thin woman standing behind the counter, and no other patrons. Silver and gold flashed under a bank of lighting, while dark velvet curtains contrasted in heightened elegance with the shimmer of diamonds and the milky gleam of pearls.

Melissa's mother had never liked diamonds. She preferred splashy, colorful stones, glass beads, and jewelry from obscure artists in SoHo. Melissa, on the other hand, had always had a secret fantasy—probably created by watching *Breakfast at Tiffany's* one too many times—of someday picking out a diamond ring with her fiancé.

He'd stare at her adoringly and choose an enormous stone he could barely afford.

She'd smile, bat her lashes, and hold out her hand.

They'd lose themselves in each other's eyes. A saleswoman would have to clear her throat to get their attention.

"This way, Ms. Bencher."

Ten's deep voice brought her out of her Audrey Hepburn–inspired reverie. She followed Ten's lead past the jewelry case into a small, private room with no windows and three burgundy armchairs arranged around a table. A security guard closed the door gently behind them. On the table, a black cloth appeared to conceal a square object.

"Why don't you have a seat?" Garth said.

He pulled out a chair, and she forced herself to smile and look relaxed. "Thanks, *darling*," she replied sweetly, fluttering her lashes.

He wanted this to be real? Then, damn it, he was going to have to deal with *her* reality. The one where people got married because they liked each other. Cared about each other. Maybe even loved each other.

On impulse, she leaned over and kissed him lightly on the cheek. He froze. She patted his hand and tried to act nonchalant.

Did I really just kiss my boss?

Her small, rebellious gesture had clearly backfired, as the touch of her lips against his skin sent a shock of heat racing through her body.

"I had Ten bring out a few pieces I thought you'd like," Garth said, his voice slightly strangled. A moment later, he forced out, "Sweetheart."

She slid into one of the chairs and ran her palms down the soft velvet upholstery. Garth sat down beside her and took her hand. He squeezed gently. The gesture was obviously intended to communicate a casual *Isn't this fun?* to Ten, and a terse *Don't mess with me, baby* to her.

She squeezed back, hoping to convey her own mix of *I love you, too, darling*, and *If you dish it out, you better be ready to take it.*

"Let's see what you've got, Ten," Garth said, nodding toward the large man across from them.

Ten pulled the cloth off the table with a flourish, revealing a silver tray with a black velvet ring display on top. Five diamonds winked at Melissa, and she gasped.

"Now that's exactly the sort of reaction I was hoping for," Ten said, with a deep chuckle.

The diamonds were huge, and they twinkled madly as living rainbows danced across their surface. Each stone had its own shape and character. Ten began to describe the different cuts—Melissa heard the words "heart," "marquis," and "emerald." But she couldn't focus on anything other than the rings and the feeling of Garth's hand, warm and solid against hers.

"Why don't you try one?" Ten said. "They transform when

they're on your hand. You'll see." He handed Garth a ring with a large center stone set high above a delicate platinum band.

Garth let go of her other hand to take the ring from Ten. He held it between his thumb and forefinger. "Ready?" he asked, his eyes locking onto hers.

Melissa nodded. Nerves suddenly tightened her stomach. She knew this was all make-believe, but somehow, that didn't quite matter.

Garth reached for her left hand. She tried to look excited and relaxed all at once. She guessed it didn't work, as her cheeks flushed with the sudden beating of her heart.

The heavy metal slipped onto her finger. Garth lingered, holding her hand in his. He stroked her palm. Melissa quivered, deep in her stomach.

"What do you think?" Garth asked.

She stared at her hand. The huge stone sat there, winking at her. It was a magnificent piece of jewelry and she should have been excited, on some purely feminine level, to wear it. But when she looked at her finger and saw how the enormous jewel swallowed up most of her hand, it felt…wrong.

She glanced at Garth. "I—I don't know," she replied, unsure how to react.

He studied her hand. He lifted it up slightly, and turned it an inch or so in either direction. Then he looked into her eyes and Melissa had the feeling he was reading her mind.

"No," Garth said. He slid the ring off her finger. "Not right."

Melissa breathed a sigh of relief, even while she felt an odd sense of loss when he broke off the contact between them.

They tried two others, but each time, Garth studied the ring, studied Melissa, and then declared it a failure. Finally, he leaned toward Ten and whispered something in his ear. Ten nodded approvingly and walked behind a small counter. He bent down and retrieved something from underneath.

"I brought it just in case," he said, as he handed a small black box to Garth.

The box opened with a soft *click*. Garth stared inside for a moment before withdrawing the tiny object. As they had each time before, Garth gently slipped the new ring on her finger. Melissa looked down, fearing another huge diamond.

And then froze.

This ring was entirely different from the others. A large, aquamarine stone sparkled from the center, circled by what had to be twenty or thirty tiny, shimmering diamonds. Delicate filigree danced around the stones, giving the whole thing an otherworldly, ornate beauty. It was lighter than the other rings, but taller.

"It's one of our vintage rings," Ten said. "An Art Deco piece from the 1920s. Recently discovered at an estate sale. There were a few missing stones that had to be replaced, but otherwise, it's all original period work."

"It's incredible," Melissa breathed. She traced the outline of the center stone with one finger. The ring felt magical, like she'd just been given a treasure from a fairy tale. She imagined the original owner as a slightly built woman with a sleek cap of shining hair, wearing the ring with her waist-long string of pearls and flapper dress.

She glanced up from the ring and her gaze was captured by Garth, who was staring at her with an uncanny intensity.

"What?" she asked hesitantly.

Garth paused, and Melissa felt a blush rising in her cheeks. She brushed back a strand of hair and laughed weakly, staring at her hand. "Do you like it?"

"I do." He reached out and tipped her face toward his. "It's perfect."

Melissa looked up, surprised to feel his hand on her skin. Any protest died on her lips as Garth leaned forward and silenced her with a kiss.

...

He'd done it on impulse, a crude means of exerting some sort of revenge on Melissa for flustering him. He'd wanted to punish her for the little kiss she'd planted on his cheek, which had stopped him in his tracks, and the bizarre spark of connection he'd felt each time he touched her skin and slipped a new ring on her finger. He shouldn't feel anything at all, and instead he felt a surge of possessive pleasure at the act of marking and branding her as *his*, wearing *his* ring.

The whole experience was barbaric and chauvinistic and utterly unlike him. He'd thought about Samantha for the barest second when he slipped on the first ring, but she was forgotten in a heartbeat. Because Melissa was different, and something about the look on her face when he slid on the final ring erased the memories that he'd been nursing for years.

And then his body took over for his mind and he leaned forward without only the barest moment of hesitation.

The need was too intense, the moment too right.

Melissa froze as they touched, her lips parting under his. They merged for one moment, and he could smell her hint of roses, taste of mint, and softness all delivered through the silky warmth of her lips. He touched her lip with his tongue. Her mouth parted and he pressed his advantage, exploring and tasting, not even caring that Ten was there, or that security cameras were likely recording the entire interaction. All he knew was a fierce desire to linger, to lose himself in a tempest of heat and need.

She seemed to feel the same, eagerly responding,

matching his movements with her own. He touched the back of her neck, tickled the silky hair that had been pulled into a loose knot. He wanted to unleash it. Drag it down and tangle his hands in it.

He wanted to hold tight. Explore her curves. Claim her.

It was the very intensity of his desire that finally drew him back.

Hellfire.

This wasn't how it was supposed to go.

With an effort, he concealed the moment of unrestrained emotion. Melissa's eyes were wide, her lips parted in surprise. Had she felt it, too?

Unsure of the answer, he forced a small, satisfied smile, as if he'd done the whole thing just to irritate her. As if the exercise of slipping rings on her finger and then kissing her soundly didn't affect him in the least.

Her eyes flared with anger, and he relaxed. That was better. He would rather she was angry with him and thought that he had used her than have her know how deeply that single kiss had affected him. After all, the last thing he wanted was to give her the impression that any of this—anything at all—was real. He didn't want, or need, a bride. He'd built his life around the expectation of being alone, and he was happy with that.

Or, at least, satisfied.

"It's perfect for you," he said. "Just perfect."

"You know me so well," she replied sweetly, her eyes stabbing him like knives. She made a point of turning away from him, gently stroking the edges of the ring and positioning her hand at various angles to see how the tiny diamonds caught the light.

Garth turned to Ten. "Thanks for bringing that one out."

"Of course, Mr. Solen," Ten replied, nodding with pleasure

as he studied Melissa and the ring. "You obviously know your lady. Those others didn't do her justice. This is perfect."

Garth watched the hint of pink in Melissa's cheeks deepen under Ten's regard. The soft color emphasized the delicate curves of her face, and the deep blue of the stone accentuated the cerulean cast of her eyes.

"I agree." His response came unbidden, and Melissa turned to him, startled.

Damn it, since when had his mouth taken control of his brain?

Ten turned to collect the other rings, and Garth hastened to drop Melissa an exaggerated bow. "Only the best for you, *darling*."

She could not hide the flash of disappointment that stole the smile from her face. Or the look of anger that followed.

A cold shiver danced along his spine. Less than a day of their "engagement" had passed, and here he was, lurching from emotion to emotion, resorting to cruel games to cover his own confusion and misplaced emotions. For the first time, Garth wondered if the entire charade could have been a big mistake.

No. Nan needs this.

He pushed aside the doubt. In three weeks, the game would be done. Nan would be better, he and Melissa would go their separate ways. Life would go on just as it had before.

She was, after all, a *fake* fiancée.

Chapter Six

Melissa awoke Saturday morning with a sore throat and a pounding headache. The sore throat came from parroting, "I know it's crazy! What can I say—we fell in love!" over and over, and the headache from taking a fresh gulp of wine every time she said it.

To her mother. Her brothers. Friends from college. Friends she didn't even know she had.

Apparently, becoming the fiancée of a billionaire made her something of a catch in New York social circles. One of the many things she hadn't considered when she'd agreed to this ridiculous charade.

Why in the name of all that's holy did *you agree to do this?*

The answer there appeared more than a little complex. Guilt? Yes, absolutely. She'd been caught in a lie and felt terrible about it. And she hated the idea of Garth's grandmother being involved. Yet there was more than just guilt involved. There was also some part of her—an embarrassed, adolescent part—that had thrilled to the prospect of spending more time with Garth, particularly such intimate time.

He thinks you're a lying, immature idiot.

And maybe you are.

A deep sigh.

A fake engagement? How in the world are you going to pull this off?

Then there were the other glasses of wine she'd drunk in an effort to forget that single, devastating kiss. Apparently, pretending to be Garth's fiancée was going to require self-control of epic proportions. Hating him, which she had decided to try after his mocking look on the way out of Hadrien, couldn't hurt.

Anything was better than the *"Take me, I'm yours"* response she'd given to his kiss.

Her phone rang and she rolled over, squinting at the blinking object with sleep-crusted eyes. She fumbled with the receiver until her clumsy fingers located the talk button. "Hello?"

"You ready? I'll be there in five."

Melissa cringed. They were meeting Garth's grandmother that morning. Because she didn't have a car, Garth had promised to pick her up. But he was ten minutes early. Ten minutes she desperately needed for a cup of coffee and a shower.

"Drive around," she said, wishing she had the energy to sound resolute. "I'll be ready in fifteen."

"You'll be ready in ten," he replied. "I'll pull up in front. I think there are reporters, so be prepared."

He hung up, and Melissa groaned. Garth Solen the fiancé was just as much a force of nature as Garth Solen the boss.

Ten minutes later, a cup of coffee in her hand, a large pair of sunglasses covering her eyes, and four ibuprofen in her veins, she emerged from her apartment. Garth was waiting by the front door, looking heartbreakingly gorgeous in a pair of faded jeans and casual polo shirt. Two men with cameras flashed pictures as they hurried down her short flight of steps and into the car.

"So," she said as soon as he pulled away from the curb. The presence of the reporters had unnerved her almost as much as the feeling of Garth's body, mere inches away as he shielded her from the cameras, and she had to consciously adopt a breezy, casual tone to cover her discomfort. "Any last-minute instructions before I meet Grandma? Anything I should be prepared for? A casual groping, perhaps?"

She deliberately squashed the red-hot desire that had electrified her the instant her gaze fell to his lips, and the feeling of *want* that had set every nerve tingling when she smelled his hint of spice and sandalwood.

"If you're referring to what happened yesterday, I was trying to act engaged," Garth said, as he checked his side-view mirror and merged into traffic, not the slightest hint of regret in his voice. "What engaged man doesn't kiss his bride after he finds her the perfect engagement ring?" He looked pointedly at her lap. "You do know I'll want that back, I hope."

Melissa glanced down and realized she'd been involuntarily caressing the cool surface of the aquamarine stone. "Of course," she said, even though she'd spent most of the night obsessively admiring the gorgeous thing that had taken up residence on her hand. "But in light of yesterday's incident, I think we need to set some ground rules for our little masquerade going forward."

"Oh?" Garth quirked a brow. "Like what?"

"Like no more kissing." Melissa had replayed that kiss a thousand times over the last twenty-four hours, and one thing had become perfectly clear: it could not happen again. With the simple pressure of his lips and deliberate stoking of his tongue, Garth had teased, promised, and set her body yearning. In short, he'd given her an experience she did *not* want to repeat.

Not when his smile afterward had told her that he absolutely did not feel the same.

"Sorry," Garth said, not sounding the least bit so. "That's a negative. You're my fiancée. I have to be able to kiss you whenever I want."

Melissa gritted her teeth. Great. Now he'd kiss her because he *knew* it irritated her.

"Fine," she muttered. "But only in public. And I draw the line at kissing. No other, ahem, *touching*."

"Wrong again," he said. Her dour mood seemed to be having the opposite effect on him, as his voice grew increasingly cheerful. "I need access to the torso."

"Why?" Melissa demanded.

"October 29 is the annual Autism Advocates charity auction. The press will be there and they will want to see us acting like a couple. Which may involve some posing. And touching."

She ignored the reference to touching and focused instead on the rest of his statement. "You're going to the auction?"

"Natalie Orelian is a sponsor. It's the perfect opportunity to talk to her."

Now *that* was dedication. Melissa had volunteered for the Advocates charity auction for years and it was a huge, lavish affair designed to appeal to New York's wealthiest. Tickets were a thousand dollars each, and the live-auction items ranged from original art to jewelry to haute couture clothing, donated by New York designers. Reporters swarmed the place before, during, and after. For a private person like Garth it would be a nightmare.

"Why do I need to go?" She tried to picture walking into the gala with Garth, wearing her sparkly new engagement ring. The image simply didn't compute. On the rare occasion

Garth attended a public event, he inevitably appeared with a lanky, expressionless model or a brilliant but cold heiress. Not a painfully average-looking engineer with a distinct lack of suitable evening attire.

"I had planned to bring a different date," Garth explained. "But—"

"That would be awkward," Melissa concluded, "now that you're engaged."

"Exactly."

Melissa tapped her finger against the armrest and considered the proposition. She couldn't think of any reasonable excuse for saying no. "Fine. I'll attend. And I give you permission to touch me while we're there. But above the waist only, got it?"

Garth's eyes gleamed. "Got it." He paused as they turned onto a smaller, two-lane highway. "Unless, of course, you go somewhere else first."

"What?" Melissa straightened so abruptly the seatbelt locked and held her rigidly in place. She forced herself to relax and sink back down so she could loosen the strap's death grip on her shoulder and hip. "Excuse me?"

He shrugged, and she thought she caught a hint of a tiny, genuine smile. "I'm just saying it's tit for tat." At her outraged look, his mouth actually quirked up at the corner. "Bad choice of words. All I'm saying is that I might not be the only one doing the groping. And fair's fair, right? You go below the waist, I can, too."

"That's not going to happen," Melissa said darkly.

"Of course not," Garth said.

"Why do you say it like that?" she demanded.

"What?" He cast her a quick look, all wide-eyed innocence. "I'm *agreeing* with you."

"Hmph." Melissa took a long sip from her cup of coffee.

"Why are you in such a good mood, anyway? Did Solen Labs end up on the cover of *Artificial Intelligence Today* or something?"

"Better. Orelian sent me an email congratulating me on my engagement. And she wants to see a draft funding agreement."

"Really?" Melissa turned to him in surprise.

"Apparently she's a romantic at heart." Garth's pleasure was obvious in the smooth cadence of his voice. "Now I just have to convince her to fund ThinkSpeak before you walk away and break my heart."

Chapter Seven

It took a little over forty minutes to get to Garth's house in Scarsdale. Melissa kept her face carefully impassive as they passed through a large iron gate and wove down a long driveway. The last thing she wanted was to give Garth the satisfaction of ooh-ing and aah-ing over the ancient, spreading oak trees and expansive green lawns of his—well, his *estate*.

His enormous, spectacular estate.

She knew she was unlikely to maintain the façade. Melissa's brothers had always teased her for her inability to hide her true feelings, whether they were horror at the sight of an ugly shawl her mother had found for her at a thrift store in The Village, or heartbreak when the boy she liked in high school referred to her as "one of those chess club geeks."

Melissa was, as they said, "an open book." And Garth, she was quickly realizing, was astonishingly wealthy.

Though Brit had made them all quite comfortable when he took Excorp public three years before, Melissa hadn't grown up with money. Even after Excorp became profitable, she'd always deposited her share of the family fortune directly into an investment account. It wasn't that she didn't want the money—she fully intended to use it as a trust fund for her kids, if she was ever lucky enough to have any—but she refused to let herself become dependent on it. Melissa had spent her whole life living in the shadow of her successful older brothers, and once she'd had the opportunity to make her own way in the world, she'd left New York and vowed not to come back until she was just as successful as they were.

And look how well that *turned out…*

Melissa pushed the dark thought from her head and focused on her surroundings. Regardless of how much Brit had made, the Bencher family fortune couldn't begin to rival this. After driving through what had to have been acres of green lawns, dotted with enormous old trees, the gardens began. It was October, so there was nothing in bloom, but throughout the carefully tended beds there were low shrubs with fiery red leaves mixed with spreading evergreens, and all around them were soaring maples, birches, and oaks dusting the sky with their mix of sunset-colored leaves. Melissa wasn't a real estate expert by any means, but she knew there weren't many properties, even in Scarsdale, with grounds like this.

Finally, the driveway curved around to give Melissa her first view of the house. She could barely stifle an indrawn breath at the beautiful sight. The graceful old Colonial-style structure had pristine white siding and crisp black shutters, with a wide brick path leading to a columned front porch. The house had the feeling of early America in the simple design and multi-paned windows, yet had obviously been updated for twentieth-century luxury.

Garth slowed to a stop beside the entrance to the brick walkway and turned off the car. "Before we go in," he said, "I have a few ground rules of my own."

Melissa deliberately turned away, peering into the side view mirror to fluff her bangs. "I don't think I like your rules."

Garth ignored her protest. "You are about to meet two people. One is Nan. She really wants to believe this whole engagement story, so she shouldn't be too hard to convince. Her mind is still sharp, but she does get confused sometimes. She's eighty-five, and the pneumonia has taken a toll on her. She's quite fragile, really, though she refuses to believe it."

Melissa nodded, suddenly contrite. "I understand. And I'm sorry. That must be hard for you."

He blinked, as if not expecting her sympathy. "Yes. Well, thank you, but it's fine." Seeming slightly flustered, he brushed past the moment. "At any rate, the other person you'll meet is Jessalyn."

Melissa waited. "Aaand...?"

"She's going to be a little grumpy this morning. I haven't seen her since this all went down yesterday and I didn't want to call her about it last night because I knew she'd give me hell."

Before Melissa could ask exactly *who* the grumpy Jessalyn was, or why Garth didn't want to make her mad, he leaned over her lap to peek out the passenger side window of the car. Then he leaned back and swore.

"Sorry, no time to explain. She's come out to meet the car. Just be strong and don't show any weakness."

With that dire statement, he threw open his door and jumped out.

Don't show any weakness?

Melissa took a deep breath and got out of the car. A woman was walking toward them, moving at a significant clip. She couldn't have been more than twenty-five and had short hair dyed hot pink at the ends. She wore ripped jeans and a white button-down shirt tied in a knot at the waist. The angry flare of her pierced nose and the position of her tattooed arms—tightly crossed over her chest—perfectly illustrated her feelings about Garth's engagement.

She didn't like it one bit.

"I guess you've heard the news?" Garth came around the back end of the car and stood beside Melissa. She felt oddly glad for his proximity, though the woman was several inches shorter than she was, and had no visible weapon.

"Is this an f-ing joke? Engaged? You?"

Garth winced. "Sorry, Jess, but it's all true."

Jess held up a cell phone and pointed it at Garth's face. On the screen, Melissa caught a look at a picture of herself emerging from Hadrien, Garth's arm curved protectively around her waist. She didn't even remember him touching her at that moment, probably because she had been in such a fog at the time over their mind-boggling kiss. "It's on Twitter, Garth. I heard about your engagement from Twitter!"

"Jess, I was going to—"

Garth broke off as she shook her head and then tucked the phone in her back pocket. "Whatever. I'm just the housekeeper. No reason to tell me."

"It happened fast," Garth said quickly. "I should have sent you a note last night, but I was overwhelmed with calls."

Melissa glanced at him, fascinated by the apology in his voice. This wasn't the ultra-confident boss who walked into meetings and made decisions with a single word, or the man who signed million-dollar contacts without a moment's hesitation. This was a man who didn't want to get in trouble.

Instantly, Melissa decided that she loved this pink-haired virago, with her utter and complete confidence and ability to scold Garth Solen with impunity. She vaguely reminded Melissa of Tori, albeit in pierced, tattooed sort of way.

She carefully extended her hand, fully aware that Jess's anger could come her way next. Were they really getting married, Melissa decided Jess would be an invaluable ally—

or a terrifying enemy. "I'm Melissa Bencher, the fiancée. Nice to meet you."

Jess stared, examining her inch by inch, from Melissa's simple flats and knee-length black skirt to her cherry red coat. Melissa had thrown together an outfit in a matter of minutes, and she hoped the other woman wouldn't notice the run in her hose that was slowly inching from her ankle toward her calf.

The housekeeper's gaze came to rest on Melissa's outstretched hand, and the ring sparkling on her finger. "Jessalyn Cislo."

They shook hands. Melissa winced when Jessalyn squeezed hard enough to make the ring pinch her fingers. "Nice to meet you," she said, gulping.

"Hmph." From Jessalyn's noncommittal noise, it was clear that she would decide later if she was pleased to meet Melissa or not. She kept hold of Melissa's hand and tugged just hard enough to make her stumble forward. When she was only a few inches away, Jessalyn held the ring closer to her face to examine it.

"Wait." She narrowed her gaze at Melissa, and then looked over at Garth. "Isn't that—"

"Jess," Garth's voice held a warning.

"I just noticed—" Jessalyn started to say, but then trailed off at the look in Garth's eyes.

"Why don't you keep your observations to yourself?" he suggested.

They matched stares and in an instant, Garth reasserted himself as boss. Melissa watched, fascinated, dying to know what they were talking about.

Jessalyn looked away first. "Way to overreact," she muttered under her breath. With an obvious about-face, she said in a formal tone, "Will you be needing lunch, *sir*?"

"Yes, something light," Garth replied, ignoring the sarcasm. "Do you know if Nan's awake?"

"She just finished her morning nap. Nurse Margaret is with her." Jess raised her nose in the air and stomped off toward the house. That was when Melissa noticed her combat boots. And the pink socks that matched the tips of her hair.

"I think she likes you," Garth offered.

Melissa turned to look at him. "Are you kidding?"

"She didn't kill us," Garth replied. "That says a lot."

Jessalyn stopped at the front door. She opened it a few feet, and three small whirlwinds of fur and legs rushed out and ran down the path at an astonishing speed. When they arrived at the end of the path, they leaped in the air at Garth's feet.

Melissa's mouth dropped open. In all her fantasies about her boss, she'd never imagined him surrounded by little white dogs. "Um, wow," she breathed.

Two of the dogs were barking with apparent joy, while one sat down and howled, then resumed jumping. At the sound of her voice, the howler broke away and bounded to her side. It had silky white hair that partially covered its eyes, and a pink, panting tongue. When she crouched down to pet it, the dog leaned into her hand for a moment before flopping onto its back for a tummy rub.

Garth bent over to pet one of the two dogs that continued begging for his attention. "Han, Luke, enough." At his warning tone, they stopped barking, but continued to leap with increasing fervor. Finally, he picked up the smaller of the two—a brown and white ball of squirming hair and legs—and held it in his arms. The dog immediately settled down with what Melissa could only describe as a smile on its face.

"What kind of dogs are they?" she asked.

Garth scowled at her. "Havanese. They're Nan's dogs."

"Of course they are," she said gravely.

"They are!"

"I can see that," Melissa said. She'd never heard of the breed before, but they had long muzzles with dark noses, and when they stood, their tails waved behind them like cheerful flags. None of the three looked much more than ten pounds, though it was hard to tell with all that hair. "And their names are Han and Luke?"

"The other one is Chewbacca," Jessalyn called, as she made her way back toward them. "In case you were wondering."

"You're a *Star Wars* fan," Melissa said with a smile. "I should have known."

"Nan named them, not me," Garth said, a trifle defensively.

"He's lying, isn't he?" Melissa asked Jessalyn.

The other woman shook her head. "I need to keep my job. I'm not saying a word."

"Smart move," Garth said. "Nan's obsessed with rescuing strays," he said, in what seemed to Melissa to be an obvious attempt to change the subject. "These three were born at a puppy mill that was closed because of the inhumane conditions. The dogs were in terrible condition, so of course Nan had to step in." He put down the dog he'd been holding and picked up the other one, who immediately tried to lick him in the face. Garth carefully held the happy creature so its tongue could not reach him. He petted the dog behind the ears for a moment before setting it back on the ground.

Jessalyn snorted. "I'll take *Nan's* dogs for a little walk. You two go ahead in." She whistled and started walking toward the back of the house. With one last longing look in Garth's direction, the white blobs of fur ran off behind her.

Melissa stifled a giggle as they walked through the front door. Garth and small white fluffy dogs? If she'd read it in a tabloid, she never would have believed it.

"They're sweet."

"They're ridiculous," Garth groused. "They don't deserve to be called dogs."

"Clearly, they are beneath you." Melissa snickered. "I mean, literally. Since they're the size of hamsters."

Garth glared at her as they walked through the front door. "I'll have you know Luke weighs eleven pounds."

Melissa paused. "Right. That would be a really big hamster. Guinea pig, maybe? Rabbit?"

Garth stopped to set his keys on a marble pedestal table by the door, and Melissa completely forgot about the dogs as she took in the beauty of the house. The front foyer had a white marble floor leading to a huge, curving staircase at the far end. Smooth, highly polished wood floors ran in every other direction as far as she could see, and a rich, lemony scent permeated the air. On one side of the entry lay a formal sitting room, with several brocade, stiff-backed chairs, a Queen Anne sofa, and a thick Oriental rug. On the other side of the hall was a formal dining room, with a mahogany table and crystal chandelier. In every direction, the sun sparkled through multi-paned windows.

This, at least, she had expected—a breathtaking mansion, filled with priceless antiques and works of art. The little white dogs and bossy housekeeper, not so much.

They proceeded down a hallway that lay to one side of the staircase. Garth waved toward the left as they walked past an arched entryway. "Kitchen and great room are over there, along with the sun porch, my office, and the library. Bedrooms are on the second floor. Nan's rooms are in back."

Every piece of furniture and art seemed to fit together seamlessly. The style was traditional and muted, but woven rugs, vases filled with flowers, and huge oil paintings provided spots of color that tied everything together.

For an apartment dweller, the house seemed to reverberate with space and silence. Although her building mostly housed other professionals, Melissa's next-door neighbor liked to play opera while he prepared dinner, and the resident in the apartment above her engaged in some kind of high-impact aerobics every night at eight—or at least that was what it sounded like. Not to mention that the only natural light entering her apartment came from two small windows in the combination living room/kitchen/study/dining area that represented 350 feet of her 600 square-foot apartment. Melissa could feel her shoulders dropping and some knot in her stomach untying as she eased through the beautiful space.

"You have an incredible home," she said, trying not to think about the final piece of their journey, and the woman at the other end of the hall. After meeting Jess, Melissa figured all bets were off. Garth's grandmother could be a domineering matriarch or a flighty old heiress. At this point, nothing would surprise her.

"Thank you," Garth replied, sending her a quick look as if to gauge her sincerity. "I bought it about five years ago. We updated a few things, but mostly left it as it was. The main house is almost one hundred years old, though Nan's rooms are a more recent addition."

"Has she always lived with you?"

"No. She prefers to live on her own. Or, I suppose, she *preferred* to live on her own. Until the pneumonia. Even she couldn't fight this one. They had her in the hospital for almost a week."

Melissa shot him a sideways glance. Though his expression had not changed, she was learning to identify the restrained emotion in his voice. The terse note spoke volumes about the pain the situation had caused. "She must have been glad to get out of there."

Garth paused to adjust a painting that, to Melissa's eyes, appeared perfectly straight. "The doctors wanted to keep her, but being at the hospital was making her sicker than the pneumonia. Nurses and doctors always coming and going. Noise, bright lights. No view of anything green and beautiful. And of course, no dogs. I think she misses them more than anything else."

She nodded in understanding. "Before my niece was born, my sister-in-law Felicity had to spend a couple of weeks in the hospital with preeclampsia. She said the labor was easier than the hospital stay. She described it as a weird combination of being lonely and crowded, all at the same time."

Garth shot her a surprised look. "That's exactly what Nan said. She said if I didn't get her released, she was going to walk out of there herself. And damned if she wouldn't have tried it, too."

"No place like home, I suppose." Melissa stopped for a moment to admire a delicate Chinese vase. "My apartment isn't much, but I must admit, I've grown pretty attached to it."

"How long have you been there?" Garth asked.

"Just a year. It reminds me of our old house in Queens." She smiled at the memory. "Everyone else in the family hated it because it was drafty and cold in the winter and hot and stuffy in the summer, but I loved that place. I liked to imagine the other kids who had lived there before me, and what their lives might have been like."

"Do your parents still live there?" Garth asked.

"No, they sold the place when my dad retired. Now they have a little condo in SoHo. They like it because it's close to museums and the art scene. But it's not the same."

She remembered how she'd cried when her dad told her that he'd sold the house. It had been one of their few fights—

she'd felt betrayed by her parents' failure to warn her that he was selling. She was already out of the house at the time, finishing up graduate school, so it wasn't like they needed her permission. But she'd have bought the place in a heartbeat, if given the opportunity. Knowing it was gone felt like losing a piece of her childhood.

"You miss the old place," Garth supplied.

She nodded, blinking back an unexpected wave of melancholy. "I do. What about you? Do you miss the house you grew up in?

"I moved a few times," Garth said. "It wasn't the same."

Though his tone was dismissive, Melissa recalled with a wince that his parents had died when he was young. No wonder he was so attached to his grandmother.

They continued walking, stopping at the end of the hall. Garth rapped gently on a white-framed door. Melissa steeled herself. She was about to meet the woman he would, apparently, do anything to protect. She tried to picture an 85-year-old version of Garth who believed the stories she read in tabloids and loved little white dogs, but the picture wouldn't compute. Then again, the deeper Melissa got into this house, the less any of this computed.

"Come in," a high-pitched voice replied.

Garth opened the door to an expansive room, dominated on one end by an adjustable bed and a collection of red-eyed, blinking machines. A middle-aged woman—presumably the nurse—leaned over the bed, obscuring Melissa's view of his grandmother, while a blood pressure machine beeped beside them. On the far end of the room, a set of French doors and a bank of windows looked out onto a veranda, gardens, and what appeared to be a swimming pool.

"No more talking," the nurse reproved her patient. "It throws off the results."

"Is everything okay?" Garth asked immediately.

"Fine," the nurse replied, sounding as if she'd answered that question many times before. She wore a pair of thick-soled sneakers, white pants, and a multi-colored hospital scrub shirt. "Just doing the vitals."

The machine gave a long *whoosh* and the nurse removed a Velcro arm cuff from her patient. "One fifty over ninety. That's what you get for having two cups of coffee, Mrs. Solen."

"I'm an old woman," a high-pitched, querulous voice replied. "If I want an extra cup of coffee, I'm going to have it."

The nurse rolled her eyes. "She's all yours," she said to Garth.

Melissa hadn't realized that Garth had reached out to grab her hand until they were connected. He led her to the side of the bed.

"Nan," he said. "This is Melissa Bencher. My fiancée."

Chapter Eight

Garth's grandmother sat upright in an adjustable bed. Her snowy hair had been carefully arranged into waves around her face, and she wore a simple white nightgown. Two spots of color flushed the apples of her cheeks, which were otherwise pale ivory. Her gray-blue eyes were sharp and focused, though her body appeared undeniably fragile.

Her smile—a stark contrast to her grandson's tight-lipped grimace—could not have been more welcoming. Melissa tumbled straight in love with her gentle countenance.

"Ah, Melissa." Nan leaned forward, gesturing for her to approach. "What a thrill to meet the woman who has stolen my grandson's heart. Come closer and let me have a look at you."

Melissa felt a sudden jolt of nervousness. Would the truth be written on her face?

She tugged on Garth's hand so he would accompany her to his grandmother's bedside. "I'm pleased to meet you, Mrs. Solen."

"Oh my, call me Nan, dear!" She laughed, which set off a round of coughing. Her thin shoulders hunched, and Melissa shot a quick look at Garth, who had fixed a stare on his grandmother. The cough sounded deep and painful, though as soon as she recovered, Nan pulled herself upright and slapped a smile on her face.

"Do you want something to drink?" Garth asked. "Should we come back later?"

His expression barely changed, but Melissa couldn't miss the dark flash of fear in his eyes. He might hide his emotions behind a mask, but it was not impenetrable.

"Oh Lord, no! I've been waiting for this day for years. I'm not going to miss it for a little cough. I'm just sorry I couldn't get out of bed." She touched the front of her nightgown and smiled at Melissa in apology. "You'll have to forgive me for my informal attire."

Melissa took in the wide, beaming smile, which showed no hint of hesitation or doubt, and immediately felt a stab of guilt.

Dear God, how could they lie to this woman?
On the other hand, how could they not*?*

"Please," Melissa said. "No apologies necessary."

Nan's gaze dropped to Melissa's left hand. "Is that… would you mind…"

Melissa laughed at her obvious intent. "Of course not." She held out her hand for inspection.

Nan gave a happy sigh as she leaned over and examined the ring. "It's absolutely beautiful." She looked up at Garth, and Melissa saw a glimmer of tears in her eyes. "Where did you find it?"

"Ten," Garth said.

Nan smiled. "I met Tennyson years ago," she said. She gripped Melissa's hand tightly in her own. "He was working for some other store back then, and he helped me pick out a watch for Garth for his twenty-first birthday. Garth asked him for help finding a brooch for me and they've been working together ever since. Every year, they find something special for me for Christmas. Just like my Arthur used to, when he was alive." She cast a fond glance at Garth. "It's terribly extravagant, but—"

"But you love it," Garth finished.

"I do." She rubbed the side of her thumb across the face of Melissa's ring. Her fingers were gnarled and twisted, arthritic knuckles protruding from the delicate skin. "And it's perfect for your fiancée." She turned to Melissa. "Please, sit down."

Melissa sank into a comfortable armchair beside the bed as Nan continued. "Now, you'll think me terribly nosy, but I'm hoping you'll tell me all about how you and Garth met and fell in love. It must have been so sudden!"

A rush of heat burned Melissa's cheeks. "Well…" She hesitated for a moment, half-hoping that Garth would break in with the story. When he did not, she fumbled ahead. "We, ah, work together. Garth hired me about three months ago to work at Solen Labs."

Nan nodded. "I read that in the *Star Herald*. I think that makes perfect sense, frankly. I've never understood why people say that a woman shouldn't marry her boss. Why not? They've got a lot in common."

"I believe that's called sexual harassment these days, Nan," Garth observed dryly.

"Pish," Nan said, with a dismissive wave. "You could never harass anyone."

"You can tell that to the jury."

Nan ignored him and gazed back at Melissa. "And you must be smart if he hired you. He doesn't suffer fools gladly, does he?"

Melissa chuckled. "No, that's for sure."

"But it is rather unusual for him to date someone from

work," Nan said. She turned to Garth, her eyes dancing with excitement. "Tell me, when did you know she was the one?"

Garth paused just long enough for Melissa to squirm. They probably should have practiced answers to these sorts of questions. It would only take a few mistakes for the press—and her family—to start asking questions.

"Right from the start," Garth said. "I tried to keep it professional, but we had a few late nights at the office, and then got to talking…" He shrugged. "The rest is history."

Melissa wanted to roll her eyes at his uninspired telling. That was supposed to explain a whirlwind, three-month romance? The man had absolutely no imagination.

She leaned toward Nan with a mischievous grin. "I don't care what people say, your grandson is a true romantic. For weeks he's been showering me with gifts. Flowers, chocolates—even a robotic vacuum cleaner! And then there were the romantic evenings, the private dinners at restaurants, all carefully orchestrated to keep it a secret. Garth was worried if the press got involved it would ruin everything. He's everything a girl could ask for. Isn't that right, sweetheart?"

Garth cleared his throat. "Of course. Anything for you."

"You didn't let *anyone* know?" Nan asked. She was practically twitching with excitement.

Melissa sighed. "You can't imagine how hard it was—I almost died trying to keep it to myself. Being in the office together and pretending to be all business was the worst. But we made up for it when we were alone." She fluttered her lashes at Garth. "Tell her about that thing you did."

Garth sent her a dark look. "What thing?"

"You know, that wonderfully romantic night when you kidnapped me and took me on your private jet. Tell her about it."

He did *have* a private jet, didn't he?

"Oh, *that* night." Garth came to stand behind her. He leaned down to whisper in her ear, so quietly Nan could not have heard, "You'll pay for this later, you know."

His warm breath tickled her neck. She ignored the quiver in her stomach and smiled back at him in vindication. "Don't worry," she said in a loud stage whisper. "You don't have to be embarrassed."

Nan clapped her hands together. "What did he do?"

"I flew us to the Bahamas for the weekend," Garth said. "I reserved a private villa right on the beach. It was a little over the top, I know, but I couldn't resist."

"He was so nervous," Melissa said to Nan, "when we got to the airport he was practically shaking. He really thought I might not like it! How silly can one man be?"

"You're his true love," Nan said, lowering her voice to a conspiratorial whisper. "Of course he was nervous."

Garth squeezed her shoulders. "But enough about me, sweetheart. Remember that incident with your bathing suit?" He winked at Nan. "They don't make them like they used to, I suppose."

Nan giggled. "And how did he propose?" she asked Melissa.

Melissa faltered. She glanced over at Garth. He crossed his arms over his chest, daring her to make up another story. His eyes lingered for just a moment on her lips, and Melissa had a sudden imagine of lying beside him on a beach. The warm sun on their bodies. A cold drink in her hand. Him rolling over for a long, slow kiss…

Flustered, she turned back to Nan. "It just happened," she said quickly. "We were having dinner at my place. It had been a hard day and we were talking about taking a vacation together, maybe renting an apartment in Paris, or lounging on a beach in Mexico. On impulse, I opened a bottle of champagne I'd had in the cupboard for years, leftover from some New Year's Eve party. We toasted, and—"

She stopped, horrified to realize that she'd somehow in her nervous state she'd started describing her last dinner with Mark. As they'd toasted to their future, she'd half-expected a proposal. Instead, his phone had buzzed. She'd been left with a bottle of wasted champagne and an empty seat at the table, thanks to the "emergency" call from Deanna. The next day, she'd come home from work early and found the two of them in the kitchen.

On the table.

"And?" Nan prompted. Her shoulders rounded as a deep hacking cough briefly overwhelmed her. When the spasm had passed, she glanced over at Garth. "What happened?"

Melissa suddenly found it difficult to speak, as the dark memory stole away the levity she'd been feeling. What *had* happened to her? How had she let herself get used like that? Had she always known the truth, deep down?

Brit had never liked Mark. He hadn't complained about it openly. He didn't need to. Melissa knew from his frown that he didn't like them living together. Not that he'd been a big fan of marriage for himself at the time, but he'd been deeply suspicious of Mark's intentions, particularly because Mark was so much older than she was. The fact that Mark had been Melissa's thesis advisor, and her first serious boyfriend, hadn't helped.

Was *that* one of the reasons she'd stayed with Mark so long? Some kind of childish rebellion?

Melissa shuddered inside. Damn. She really did need a therapist.

Abruptly, she realized both Garth and Nan were staring at her. "Um, where was I?" She stared up at Garth blankly, no longer even remembering what they'd been discussing.

"The proposal," Garth prompted. "You tell it so much better than I do."

Melissa forced a happy smile and directed her words at Nan. "It was the sweetest thing. Out of nowhere he looked into my eyes and said, 'I don't just want a vacation, Melissa. I want to spend the rest of my life with you. Will you marry me?'"

Nan leaned back against the pillows, her hands clasped together. "That's lovely!" She looked at Garth. "Well done."

"Naturally," he agreed, with a modest shrug of his shoulders.

"But incomplete," Nan added.

Garth straightened. "What do you mean?"

Nan turned to Melissa. "Did he get down on one knee?"

Melissa considered. "No," she said. "Now that you mention it, he didn't."

"Did he take you somewhere beautiful? Treat you like a queen? Plan a romantic moment that you'll never forget?"

"Hmm." Melissa tapped her chin. "No. And, well…no."

"I always treat you like a queen," Garth said. "Don't I?"

"Of course you do." Melissa shared a not-so-secret eye roll with Nan. Needling Garth was doing a lot to restore her mood.

Nan sniffed at Garth. "Women have certain needs, dear. You've never been particularly good at anticipating them."

"But—"

"I'll bet you didn't even have a ring to give her."

"We just bought the ring today," Garth protested. "How could I have had a ring?"

"You get a *different* ring for the proposal," Nan said, exasperated. "Something small and simple, just so you can have it when you ask her to marry you. If you'd have asked me, you would have known that."

"Next time," Garth drawled, "I will ask you to help me plan the whole thing, Nan."

The older woman sailed on. "Don't get snippy with me, young man. I'll bet you haven't even taken her to Seesaw. You've got a lot of work to do."

"Seesaw?" Garth raised a brow in surprise. "Really?"

"Yes, really."

Melissa looked back and forth between them. She had no idea what "seesaw" meant, but it didn't matter. Nothing could be more wonderful than watching Garth Solen get taken to task by his tiny scrap of a grandmother.

"We don't have time," Garth said. To Melissa's mind, it seemed obvious that he was searching for an excuse. "We're negotiating a major deal for ThinkSpeak. Maybe after that."

"Make the time," Nan ordered, the stern voice sounding strange, coming from her angelic countenance. "You've got a hundred employees to help you with your deal. I want you to go to Seesaw. I want you on one knee. And I want pictures."

"What's 'seesaw'?" Melissa asked. Nan's insistence had flustered Garth which, Melissa had to admit, she loved to see. He hadn't been expecting this.

"It's the house where my Arthur proposed to me," Nan said. "And where Garth's father proposed to his mother. It's in Essex—a sweet place my father bought when he was young. Garth actually coined the name when he was a little boy. He loved the swing set and seesaw in the back."

"You can't really expect me to—" Garth started.

"Of course I can. I'm a selfish, demanding old woman. I can expect anything I want. And I want Melissa to visit Seesaw and have a proper proposal."

Garth ran a hand through his hair. "You're not selfish."

"I'm trying to be."

He sighed. "I'll see what I can do."

Nan dropped back into her pillows and gave him a contented smile. "I thought you would."

Chapter Nine

After spending the morning with Nan, Garth dropped Melissa back at her apartment. The phone rang as soon as she walked through the door. She checked the caller ID.

Her mother. That would be call number twenty for the day. She'd ignored the first nineteen.

"Hi, Mom," she said cheerfully into the phone. "What's up?" She tucked the phone under one ear and wandered over to the large collection of plants that sat on a table next to the living room window. While they spoke, she pinched the brown edges off of the leaves of a large spider plant.

"Did you talk to Garth yet? About Sunday brunch?"

Melissa winced. "This week won't work, Mom. I'm sorry, but he's going to have to go into the office. He needs to send some documents to an investor."

"And it has to be done tomorrow? Honey, don't you think this is all a little strange? He says he wants to marry you, and then can't even make time to meet your parents?" Phoebe's voice rose dangerously with each word.

Phoebe had never been a particularly engaged parent—she spent far too much time focusing on her own needs to attend too deeply to those of her children—yet that did not diminish her desire to be important in their lives. Sometimes, Melissa thought that the less she needed her mother, the more interested in Melissa's life she became. The story about Garth had hit her particularly hard. She now seemed to be trying to reassert her motherly importance by spending as much time as she could nagging Melissa about the engagement.

Melissa moved on to a bright blue ceramic pot with a variety of sedums. Carefully, she picked out a cluster of tiny, wilted blooms. Back when she hated to leave her apartment, taking care of these plants had soothed her. Given her something to look forward to each day. She tried not to compare her table of houseplants to Garth's ten acres of grounds.

Stupid billionaire.

"Mom, he wants to meet you. He really does. It's just a terrible time. That's why we weren't going to announce this for several weeks. He knew it would be like this. He said to apologize."

"Hmph." Clearly undeterred, Phoebe snorted into the phone. "Your father doesn't understand why Garth didn't talk to him. You might want to let him know that. I'm not trying to start off on a bad foot, honey, but Garth isn't doing himself any favors."

"Can you just give him a break? He's under a lot of stress right now. This investment he's working on is his most important project ever. I've never seen him so emotional about something before."

Surprisingly enough, that was true. Even if Garth didn't wear his emotions on his sleeve, Melissa was starting to be able to read past his mask. And based on his reaction to Natalie Orelian's email that morning, he was downright ecstatic at the prospect of securing additional funding.

Her mother blew out a long breath. "What about next weekend?"

"Maybe," Melissa evaded. "I'll check with him and see. I know he's dying to meet you. I'll let you know what we can do. 'K? I've really got to run, now—my personal trainer is coming in a few minutes. Need to get in shape for the wedding, of course!" She hung up before her mother could object further.

The phone rang again almost immediately. She answered without even looking at the screen. "Mom, I've really got to—"

"Next week, Saturday."

She stopped. Blinked. "Who is this?"

"Garth." He paused, and then spoke slowly, sounding out the words as one might to an infant. "Next week. Saturday. You and I will be traveling to Seesaw and spending the weekend there."

"Oh."

They were going to spend the weekend together?

"And Nan wants to spend a little more time with you this week. I'll pick you up in the mornings and bring you to my house."

"That's absurd," she said, head spinning at the series of commands. "What about Orelian? The Kinsey project? ThinkSpeak? Danube?" Melissa thought about the mountain of work and huge variety of projects that she had been unable to focus on since that fateful morning Garth had slipped a ring on her finger. "You can't miss that much time in the office and neither can I."

"It's just for a few days, and as Nan mentioned, I am the boss." Garth paused. "I'll reassign some of your work. People will be expecting us to take some time off. You and I both probably spend too much time in front of a computer screen anyway."

She paused, struggling to take in the now strangely cordial tone of his voice. "What if I don't want you to reassign my work?"

"Melissa."

Something about the way he said her name—slowly, patiently—communicated his simultaneous sympathy and conviction that she was being absolutely ridiculous.

"Garth," she mimicked, though doing so made her feel petty.

"I'm not going to force you to give anything up," he said. "I'm just trying to make this a little easier on both of us."

She felt her objections melting away, yet she couldn't quite bring herself to agree. "I'll keep my work. And I can take the train."

"You're *not* taking the train."

She sighed. Arguing with Garth was like arguing with a brick wall. "Fine. My mother is determined to have you over for brunch, you know. You can't avoid her forever."

"Of course I can," Garth replied lightly. "And we don't have time next weekend. We will be coming back from Seesaw on Sunday."

"Then it will have to be the weekend after that."

"But the Sunday after that is October twenty-eighth. Why bother? The whole thing will be over a few days later."

For some reason, his rational series of questions irritated Melissa more than if he had simply argued with her. "We *will* bother," Melissa enunciated through clenched teeth, "because if you don't agree to meet with them they're going to call my brother Brit, and he's going to come marching back home from Scotland and create the biggest scandal you could ever imagine."

Melissa had begged her parents and brothers not to call Brit. Her excuse was an honest one—she didn't want him to cut short his trip to Scotland. They all knew the likelihood of him flying back in a hurry if he found out about a whirlwind courtship, and no one wanted him to do that. Still, her mother's reluctance to disturb Brit didn't keep her from using him as blackmail.

He blew out an exasperated breath. "We'll have coffee."

"Brunch," Melissa said, determined not to back down. "You'll come over for Sunday brunch and pretend to be a dutiful fiancé. You'll save yourself from scandal and me from being treated like an utter idiot—for the second time in a year—by my family."

"Why would they think you're an idiot?"

"I don't have a very good track record with men." Her family's propensity for treating her like a child was another topic entirely. One she had no interest in discussing with Garth. "Look, just agree to come to brunch, all right?"

There was a long pause. Finally, "All right, ten to one, Sunday the twenty-eighth."

Melissa sighed with relief. "Great. And thanks. I appreciate it."

...

Garth hung up the phone and slammed his fist against the steering wheel. Brunch? With her parents? What was he thinking?

He revved the engine and changed lanes abruptly. Damn it, the woman had the oddest effect on him. The sound of her voice conjured up images of her mouth, which in turn brought back the taste of her lips, and his pants suddenly became uncomfortably tight. Despite the fact that he'd seen her only a few minutes before, he found himself strangely eager to see her again and had almost considered inventing an excuse to turn around and bring her back to Scarsdale right then and there.

Most confusing of all, he had, for some reason, just agreed to do the thing he hated most—socialize with a bunch of strangers—simply to make her happy. He gritted his teeth, knowing what would most likely result.

Be careful what you wish for, Melissa, he thought grimly. *You might not like what you get.*

Chapter Ten

For the next week, Garth appeared at her apartment each morning at seven and drove her back with him to Scarsdale. He had breakfast with Melissa and Nan, and then disappeared to his study to work for an hour while the women spent time looking at old photo albums, drinking tea, and talking. Melissa could already tell breaking up with Garth would be difficult when the time came—if only because she would miss his sweet grandmother, who struggled to lift the heavy books of pictures, and occasionally coughed so hard it brought tears to her eyes.

From there, they'd head to the city, where Melissa would spend a few minutes being teased by her co-workers, usually until the moment Garth would walk down the hall, at which point everyone would fall silent and hurry away to their desks. She worked furiously when she was in her office, more determined than ever to prove her worth to Solen Labs—and herself. She was not going to let one mistake ruin the rest of her career. She loved the work too much, even if it meant enduring awkward smiles and knowing looks.

Her favorite part of the day came at six when Garth

would appear at her door, with his hint of a shadow on his beard, to drive her home. Her friend Hal, who worked in the office next to hers, would give them both a jaunty salute when they walked out the door. On the way home, they'd talk about work. Garth would bounce ideas off of her, or she'd share her frustration over stubborn programming issues.

"Did you see the latest ThinkSpeak prototype?" he'd asked her one day. The excitement in his voice was more than she'd ever heard from him, and it made her smile.

"I did," she replied. "We all did. You made a point of bringing it around the office, remember?"

Garth shot her a look as he pulled out into the thick New York traffic. "I suppose I did. But I had the feeling there was something you didn't tell me. Some feedback on the design?"

Melissa paused to collect her thoughts. "I wonder if there's some way to streamline it? Make it less obtrusive? I was thinking that we might be able to redesign the sensors and create more of a cap, less of a bulky helmet. It seems like anything we can do to make these kids and their caregivers feel more comfortable in groups, the better."

Garth tapped his finger on his lips. "That's a great point. We might be able to move some of the electronics from the cap to the central processor. That could lighten things up considerably."

They brainstormed back and forth that night, and the next day as well. Meanwhile, Melissa carefully reminded herself every day that her engagement was *fake*. It was one thing to nurse an unrequited crush on her boss. It was another thing to fall for a bossy, emotionally unavailable pretend fiancé. The problem was, the more she got to know him, the harder it became to invent reasons not to like him.

For one thing, Garth was absolutely devoted to his grandmother. That was obvious. And even though his housekeeper was a tad rough around the edges, he seemed attached to her as well. Then there was his unmistakable fondness for the three dogs that followed him around like a god. It was difficult to think cruel thoughts about a man who had a weakness for little white dogs. Especially ones named after *Star Wars* characters.

Though by no means effusive, he smiled and laughed—even joked—when he was at home with Nan and Jess, something he never did in public. She had known he was intensely private, but Melissa now suspected that meant more than simply not giving out his phone number. It also meant not sharing his emotions with people he didn't trust.

Which was to say, almost everyone.

At least he's still bossy. I can still hate that about him.

There had been no repeat of the kiss that had left her reeling, and she told herself she was relieved. But when she fell asleep at night she kept imagining him leaning over her, a tiny, ineffable smile creasing the corner of his mouth just before he set her lips on fire.

• • •

Garth picked her up early Friday morning. He threw her small suitcase into the back of car and then wove his way out of Brooklyn, headed for Connecticut. He had a different car today—a black BMW coupe with a buttery-soft leather interior. Melissa hadn't slept well the night before—she was too worried about what the weekend would be like—and her nerves combined with her overtired state to create a generally foul mood.

"Is this what billionaires do?" Melissa asked, wrinkling her nose. "Switch expensive cars once a week?"

She'd discovered, earlier in the week, that needling Garth

could provide hours of amusement. Particularly when he did that little frowny thing that meant she'd gotten under his skin.

"It's about one hundred twenty miles to Essex. The Tesla has a three-hundred-mile range, but I don't like to risk it." He patted the steering wheel. "Besides, she gets antsy if I leave her in the garage too long."

Melissa's phone rang. She dug it out of her purse and checked the screen.

Perfect. Her mother. At seven a.m. on a Friday.

She bared her teeth at Garth in a feline smile. "I've been dodging my mother all week. She keeps asking me questions about you that I can't answer. Now you can suffer along with me." She pushed the button to answer. "Hi, Mom," she said brightly. "We were just talking about you. And brunch. Garth's really looking forward to it."

Beside her, the frowny face appeared.

Melissa enjoyed only a small moment of triumph before drowning in a barrage of questions. She paused every few minutes to mute her phone and turn to Garth for answers every woman should have about her husband-to-be.

Like, "Is he allergic to anything?" (Yes, tomatoes.)

"How does he feel about cats?" (Not a fan, but willing to fake it.)

"Vegetarian?" (Eye roll.)

And then came more of the other questions, the ones she'd been putting off all week, which were coming with increasing frequency and urgency. Things like: "Why can't you set a date? (This is a busy time, Mom. We can't think about that right now.) "What kind of cake do you want?" (For the love of God, Mom, can't that wait?) "Can we invite Uncle Ralph? I think he'll be out of rehab next month." (Groan. Uncle Ralph? Really?)

Then again, her mother's questions were nothing

compared to the ones that had been coming her way from her brothers. Melissa didn't like the idea of fooling her parents, but she *hated* the idea of hiding the truth from Joe and Ross. The three of them had always been close, sometimes in solidarity against Brit, sometimes against her parents. She'd never lied to them before, and doing so now nauseated her.

After twenty minutes on the phone with her mother, she pretended to lose the signal. Twice. Finally, Phoebe seemed to get the hint.

"We'll see you next Sunday! Bye!"

Melissa collapsed back into the seat and blew out a long breath.

"You look like you've just run a marathon," Garth observed. Despite all her questions, he'd managed to maintain his equanimity during the phone call. Something about her increasing irritation seemed to rub him the right way.

"My mother has a special knack for being controlling when it comes to matters that she cares about," Melissa said, "and absent when it comes to things she doesn't." She realized her words sounded harsh and sighed. "To be fair, it isn't every day you learn about your daughter's engagement in a tabloid."

"But at some point," Garth said. "She's just got to trust your judgment, right?"

Melissa laughed, though the sound held no humor. "My parents stopped trusting my judgment after I moved in with Mark. Dealing the aftermath of his cheating didn't help." She stared out at the road before them, already feeling the sting of her family's disapproval when she told them she was breaking up with Garth—three weeks after she'd announced her engagement.

Garth glanced at her and then back to the road. "What exactly happened with him?"

"He was my thesis advisor. He told me he loved me and I believed him. He asked me to come to California with him when he set up his lab, and I did. I was starry-eyed. I thought he was The One."

"And?"

"And then he cheated on me with one of the lab assistants. Everyone in our circle knew about it. And I, um, had a hard time for a while."

That is, if refusing to leave her apartment for weeks, losing fifteen pounds, and generally falling apart for nine months constituted a hard time.

"Tori mentioned that."

Melissa burrowed deeper into her seat, her cheeks burning with embarrassment. "Really? She told you I was depressed?"

His voice was surprisingly gentle. "No, of course not. All she said was that you'd had a hard go of it."

"Things got a little rough," she admitted. "My family was pretty worried about me. Looking back, I think it was about more than just Mark. I was trying to figure out who I was and what I wanted out of life, and everything just seemed so hopeless. But all Brit and the others could see was that I was depressed because the guy they'd all warned me about had made a fool out of me."

"No one made a fool out of you," Garth said, his lip curling with disgust. "The guy's a predator. I hate to say it, but he's got a terrible reputation. Even *I've* heard the rumors, and that's saying a lot."

Melissa gave him a small, sad smile. "You aren't the first person to tell me that. I probably knew, deep down, that there was something wrong with him, but honestly, it didn't matter. I wanted to get away, and he gave me the perfect excuse." She pictured Brit's disapproving look when she told him about Mark. "One of my brothers is a little, shall we say, *overprotective*. The fact that he didn't like Mark just made it all the better."

"You're talking about the guy Tori ended up with? What's his name—Brit?"

She smiled. She was so used to people knowing her brother first, it was downright delightful to have someone say his name with that sound of confusion. "Yep, that's the one. I didn't realize it at the time, but I think moving to California was my own form of an adolescent rebellion. A misguided attempt to gain some independence. It's just too bad I let myself get used by a guy like Mark to get there."

"Better than dropping out of school and getting pregnant, I suppose."

Melissa laughed. "I never thought of it that way, but I suppose you're right." Talking about Mark and Brit was giving her the strangest feeling—like she was shedding the burdens of months of self-doubt and pity. A light, relieved sensation bubbled up through her.

"What about you?" she asked. "Did you go through any rebellion? It's hard to picture rebelling against Nan."

Garth relaxed against the seat, one hand pressing lightly against the steering wheel. "She wasn't much of an authoritarian, that's for sure. If anything, it was the pressure of her thinking everything was perfect that got to me the most."

"What do you mean?"

"She just assumed I'd be class president, captain of the football team, and a Rhodes scholar. All at the same time."

"A little bit of pressure?"

"I suppose. It made her so happy to see me succeed, I didn't have the heart to tell her that I didn't have any friends, or that the kids at school thought I was odd because I'd rather read a book about computers than go out to parties." He shrugged self-consciously. "What an absurd thing to complain about."

"Make perfect sense to me," Melissa said. She stared out at the road and tried to imagine Garth in high school. Vaguely, she could imagine him as a tall, skinny adolescent. The smartest kid at the school and probably not the most popular. A far cry from the intense, perfectly controlled persona he now projected.

Silence stretched between them, and Melissa wondered if he regretted the admission. "This area is so beautiful," she said, hoping to guide the conversation to more neutral ground. An explosion of colors flanked the road, topped by the deep blue sky of a cloudless New England fall day. "Did you spend a lot of time here when you were a kid?"

"Mostly over the summers."

"With Nan?"

"With my parents first, and then with Nan."

Nice one, nosy.

"I'm sorry. I didn't mean to pry."

"It's okay." He paused. "My great-grandfather, Nan's dad, bought Seesaw as a vacation getaway for the family. Nan spent her summers here as a kid, and she brought my mom out every year as well. When I was born, my parents figured they'd continue the tradition. The summer I turned five, they decided to try leaving me with Nan so they could take a vacation. They died in a car accident on the way to the airport."

"Oh, I'm so sorry." Melissa sat in silence, unable to even begin to fathom how it must have felt for Garth and Nan to face that kind of loss. "Do you think about them when you come back here?"

He shook his head. "No. I've had a lot of time to build new memories of this place. You see, Grandpa Arthur, Nan's husband, was a doctor and he worked long hours. Nan never really liked the city, so whenever I was out of school she and I came here. She had more of a community in Essex than she did in New York."

"Did she ever think about living here full time?"

"She and Arthur were planning to live here after he retired, but he couldn't seem to bring himself to stop working. He died of a heart attack a few years ago, and with Nan's health failing, I convinced her to move to Scarsdale so I could keep an eye on her."

"When's the last time you were back?"

"It's been a while. She can't travel on her own, and I've been too busy to bring her."

"I see." Melissa's heart tugged in her chest. "No wonder she wanted us to come out."

Garth nodded, his gaze pinned on the road.

Funny, all the things a house could mean. Melissa thought about her attachment to her family home in Queens, and then how her apartment in New York, though small and noisy, had been so important for her rebuilding her sense of independence. She pictured five-year-old Garth, trying to make sense of a world without his parents, clinging to the comfort of a place he knew and loved at the same time he'd lost the most important things in his world.

And now, of course, he'd have to make peace with coming here without Nan.

The realization hit her abruptly: Garth must be preparing, on some level, to say good-bye to Nan, and he'd tangled Seesaw up in his feelings about her. That had to be why he'd avoided coming out. She knew better than anyone that his work was mobile. If he'd really wanted to come to Seesaw, he could have done so at any time.

Maybe he'd been avoiding the trip because of his memory

of losing his parents, or maybe he didn't want to face the fact that he'd have to start coming up here alone. Either way, visiting Seesaw was probably the last thing he wanted to do with Nan back at home, obviously struggling.

Melissa peeked at Garth, but his usual mask was in place as he stared at the road. She wanted to touch him, but didn't. Instead, she watched the road, and the way his fingers tightened on the steering wheel.

He cleared his throat. "I was planning to come out anyway and check on things."

"Sure." She leaned forward to adjust the radio. "Sure you were."

...

They drove into Essex Village around noon. Melissa felt a little of Garth's somber mood lift as they passed through the town center. Tightly packed, quaint old buildings of white wood and brick, with signs proclaiming their ages—1776, 1779—conspired along with the crisp fall air and faint smell of cider and cinnamon to create a picture that was almost surreal in its old New England charm.

Garth stopped so they could get a good view of the marina, with its combination of expensive yachts and fishing boats, and the Connecticut River, with sheltered coves to the north and south. They stopped at a bakery for coffee, and then bought fresh bread and apple butter. Garth took them to a tiny bookstore, where he browsed the travel books and Melissa found a paperback thriller she'd been wanting to read for months.

"New Zealand?" she said, looking at the cover of the travel guide he'd purchased. "You have plans to visit?"

"In March. I've wanted to go for years."

"*Lord of the Rings* fan, by any chance?"

Garth's mouth turned up into a sheepish half-grin. "Guilty." He lowered his sunglasses over his eyes, and checked his watch. "Did you want to do any other shopping? There are quite a few boutiques." He pointed to a windowed storefront across the street, which had a display of clothing and jewelry in the window. "Lily's Closet is very popular. You wouldn't know it from the outside, but they've got a large shoe section in the back."

"Spend a lot of time there, do you?"

"You discovered my dark secret," Garth said. "I collect women's shoes."

Melissa placed her hand over her heart, feigning shock. "I declare, Mr. Solen, did you just make a joke? About women's shoes?"

He shook his head. "If so, it was entirely unintentional."

She laughed. A couple on the other side of the street looked over at them and then turned to each other and said something under their hands. Deliberately, Melissa laced her arm through the crook of his elbow and smiled. Through her grin she said softly, "I think the locals are getting interested. We might want to head out."

He followed her gaze. A moment later, an older woman with perfectly bobbed white hair emerged from an antique store across the street and waved. "Hello, Garth dear!" she hollered, in a voice that reminded Melissa of a charging bull. "Lovely to see you!"

"Don't stop," Garth whispered. "That's one of Nan's old bridge partners—if we land in her clutches we'll never escape. Just wave and look engaged."

They waved vigorously but kept walking. Garth slipped his arm around her waist. The intimacy of the contact sent her pulse racing. Melissa was acutely aware of the imprint of his hand, the movement of his hip against hers, and the way his fingers slid against the delicate skin of her stomach. Despite the cool breeze off the water, the proximity of the lips she'd begun to fantasize about somewhere around the Connecticut border soon had her cheeks flushed with heat.

They drove about a mile out of the village before Garth pulled off Main Street onto a side street, and from there, turned into a wide gravel driveway a few houses down from the corner. "Here we are."

Like most of the houses in Essex, Seesaw looked at least a hundred years old, possibly more—a square, two-story Victorian with a wrap-around porch and glassed-in mudroom off the side door. The large grassy yard behind the house was scattered with falling red and yellow leaves, but otherwise appeared carefully maintained. The paint was fresh and bright. Melissa had no doubt Garth had the house maintained in pristine condition.

"I'm not sure it gets more charming than this," Melissa said. She glanced at Garth, wondering how he felt now that he was faced with the house.

Garth sat for a moment just looking at the small garage at the end of the driveway. He blinked a few times but otherwise remained still, revealing nothing of whatever inner battle he might have been fighting. Finally, he opened his door and got out of the car. Melissa came around and met him by the trunk.

He pointed toward the back yard as he grabbed the small box from the bakery. "There it is."

She followed his gesture, smiling when she realized what he meant. "Oh! The seesaw!"

In the far corner of the yard stood a playset of the old aluminum variety, with two swings held by rusty chains and a straight slide. The seesaw stood off by itself, a dark red plank of wood resting against a thick silver pipe

Melissa started toward the play structure. When Garth didn't immediately follow, she beckoned toward him. "What are you waiting for?"

"Nothing. I'll bring in our bags. You can come in when you're ready."

"You're not even going to check it out?"

"I can see it from here."

"It's not going to bite you."

"I'm not so sure of that," Garth replied. "Have you been on one of those things recently?"

"In fact, I have," Melissa said. "With my niece just a few weeks ago." She gestured again. "Come on. We've got to get a picture for Nan."

He followed her, holding the white bakery box in one hand. "Fine, but I'm not getting on it. You must be far more agile than I am if you still ride these things."

"I don't know about agile," she said, "but I do a lot of babysitting. It keeps me young." She stopped beside the aluminum slide, which sparkled with the reflection of the sun. "My nieces and nephews would love this place."

"How many do you have?"

"Four. My brother Ross has three, and Joe has one."

"It's been a while since anyone below the age of thirty has been out here," Garth said. "This thing would probably fall apart if they tried to play on it." He rested his free hand on top of the wooden seesaw.

"Are you so sure about that?" Melissa asked. She tugged the box from his hand and set it on the ground. "Let's try it and see."

He raised a brow. "You're kidding, I assume."

"No way." She was glad she'd worn her jeans and comfortable flats. She stepped over the far end of the seesaw, grabbed the handle, and flashed him a smile. "Come on, are you scared or something?"

Garth crossed his arms over his chest. "That is the oldest, dumbest trick in the book."

"Don't forget, I work with you," Melissa said. "I know how competitive you are."

"I'm not getting on the seesaw."

"Don't be such a fuddy-duddy," she chided.

"I am *not* a fuddy-duddy."

"Anyone who has to *say* they aren't a fuddy-duddy obviously *is* a fuddy-duddy."

"You need to stop using that word. It sounds ridiculous."

Melissa grinned. "Fuddy-duddy, fuddy-duddy!"

Garth put his hands over his ears and winced. "Fine. I'll ride the seesaw. But you'll have to watch out. I'm a bit bigger than you are."

"Don't be so cocky," she advised. "You're out of practice."

He grabbed hold of the other end of the seesaw and swung one leg over. Melissa cautiously lowered her weight onto her side, keeping her feet on the ground. But of course as she did, Garth lowered his own weight, jerking her high into the air.

"Whoa!" Melissa slipped to one side and almost lost her balance. She righted herself a moment later. "Okay, fine. You've got some skills." She bounced experimentally, but couldn't move her side any lower.

"How's it going up there?" Garth asked, cocking his head politely. "Need anything? A drink, perhaps?"

He held her easily while she flailed around, swinging her feet in the air. She bounced again, harder this time, but couldn't move him.

"Darn you, Garth Solen," she grumbled.

"What's that? Did you just say, 'Yes, Garth, you dominate the seesaw'?"

Melissa scooted to the very end of the board and bounced again. Garth didn't move. Then, deliberately, he lowered himself all the way to the ground. Melissa soared up another few feet, bounced, and then stopped.

She groaned, swinging her legs with all her might. Garth let her down a few inches, and then brought her back up with a jerk. The movement caught her mid-bounce, and she lost her balance somewhere between the sky and the smooth red wood.

"Whoa!" Melissa landed in the soft grass with a grunt. When the shock wore off, she rolled to one side and rubbed her sore bottom experimentally. Nothing broken.

"I can't believe you…" she started to speak, but as she looked up Melissa realized Garth was *laughing*. Not smirking or smiling, or even chuckling, but full out laughing.

Her heart flipped.

"Nice. Very nice." She manufactured a scowl to cover the sudden rush of emotions the sound of Garth's laughter had evoked. "I hope you're happy with yourself. I think I hurt my…" She patted the edge of her bottom. "My you-know-what."

Garth stepped off the seesaw and approached her. His dark eyes were still dancing with humor. He held out one hand. "Can I help you up? I hate to see a woman and her you-know-what on the ground."

She held out her hand and shook it demandingly. "You better help me up, you seesaw-shark."

With a smile lingering on his face, he grabbed her hand and pulled her to her feet. She lost her balance and tumbled forward, falling against him. She put out her hands to steady herself, and found herself clutching a strong, male chest.

"I'm so…sorry…" she trailed off as she looked up into his eyes.

He gazed down at her, an odd expression on his face. His lips lay together in a relaxed line. With one hand, he tucked a long strand of hair behind her ear. "You're a good sport," he said softly.

"I, uh…"

"Even if I could kill you for getting us into this mess, I have to admit that I'm glad I'm here." He held her gaze for one long moment.

Kiss me, damn it!

The words appeared unbidden in her brain.

Kiss me now!

Her unconscious shouted again, apparently determined to reach him.

He did not move. They remained pressed against each other, Melissa's hands resting against his chest, her legs touching his thighs. Heat seared along the length of their contact.

A deep longing kept her motionless, pressed against him. All that she could think was how desperately, madly she wanted him to touch her.

And then he did. And her world exploded with desire.

Chapter Eleven

He started with her lips, covering them in a gentle kiss that slowly deepened and strengthened. When he nipped at her lower lip, flames fanned from her toes to stomach. Abandoning any pretense of control, Melissa wrapped her arms around his neck and touched him with her tongue, moving against him in a silent invitation. She was rewarded with a groan, and then his arms closed around her waist.

"Melissa," he breathed, touching his lips to her jaw, the line of her neck, the delicate flesh at the hollow of her throat. "We shouldn't..."

"Shut up," she said, and she trailed her hands down his back, reveling in the length of muscles along his spine. Something about the sky and the trees and the magic of this place had messed with her brain, and she couldn't imagine not touching him.

She shouldn't want him. She shouldn't want any of this. She was rebuilding her life and her heart. An affair with Garth was the last thing she needed.

And yet...didn't she need this, too? Physical contact, the way her senses came alive when he was near? Wasn't there a price to be paid for safety as well as risk?

Shut up and stop analyzing…not everything has to make sense!

He buried his hands in her hair and dragged her closer, pulling her in, tasting her as if he could draw her inside of him through the force of his passion.

Melissa wanted to drown in his touch, in the mastery and power of it. She eased her hips into his, moving her head against his hands, wanting him to hold her even tighter, to clutch her to him with even more power.

Astonished at her own boldness, she dropped her hands lower, to rest just below the waistline of his pants. Muscles flexed there, and he ground more deeply against her.

"You went first," he muttered, and then she felt him skim his hands down the side of her rib cage, settling at her waist. With a quick, easy motion he pulled her turtleneck out of her pants and slipped his hands underneath. They rested on the soft skin of her stomach.

She arched into the touch. "Who cares," she said, her speech garbled by the fresh rush of desire between her legs. "Permission granted."

He didn't hesitate. Large, broad hands swept from her ribs to the line of her lacy bra, where they tickled the hard nubs of her nipples.

Melissa sighed and arched deeper, praying he wouldn't stop.

Pressure. All she could think was that she desperately needed more pressure.

Harder, she begged him silently.

He obliged with a thumb, lightly brushed against the hard peak. Then again, a thumb and forefinger. A gentle squeeze. The promise of more.

Her knees buckled. A soft moan emerged from her lips.

"No, that's his car, he must be here somewhere. Anyway, Janey said she saw him in town."

A male voice broke the privacy of the erotic moment. He must have been out on the street, talking to a companion. Garth froze, and then his hands disappeared from her skin. Melissa wrenched herself back to the present.

"Should we go around front?" a female voice replied.

Garth swore. "Neighbors," he growled under his breath.

"Well, hey!" The man again. "Is that you, Garth?"

With a plastered smile on her face, Melissa turned around. Garth's arm remained at her waist. She leaned into it gratefully, feeling equal parts embarrassment and frustration.

A couple who looked to be in their mid-forties made their way up the gravel driveway. The man wore a pink oxford with a logo on the breast and a pair of neatly pressed khaki pants. He had blond hair that crested in a wave at his forehead. Melissa suspected hairspray was involved.

"Howard. Yolanda." Garth nodded in greeting, his voice smooth and polite.

"Didn't mean to interrupt, but we wanted to say congratulations!" Yolanda's hair had evidently been dyed to match her husband's, and she must have used an equivalent amount of hairspray to achieve the perfect helmet that stood about three inches above the crown of her head and ended in a flip at her shoulders. She wore pink lipstick and a scarf tied in a jaunty knot at her neck.

They looked ready to set sail.

"We heard the big news." Howard smiled and continued toward them, revealing a full complement of perfect white teeth. "Couldn't believe it at first. Our Garth? A secret fiancée? Whirlwind romance?" He glanced at his companion and they both laughed. "No way!"

They reached the top of the driveway. Yolanda glanced

down at the grass and frowned. Melissa suspect her displeasure had something to do with her white flats, each adorned with a navy blue bow.

"I guess seeing is believing!" Howard guffawed and Yolanda tittered.

Garth's arm tightened around Melissa.

"No man is an island," Yolanda observed, nodding wisely. "Even our Garth."

Melissa decided if either of them used the phrase "our Garth" one more time, she would punch them in the jaw. "I'm Melissa Bencher," she said, forcing a polite smile.

"Howard and Yolanda Fendle." Howard dragged his wife over to where Garth and Melissa stood. He extended a meaty hand toward her. "Old friends of the family."

From the steely glint in Garth's eyes, Melissa suspected "friend" was a gross exaggeration.

"We met Garth when he was just a little boy," Yolanda gushed. "At sailing camp." She glanced at Howard as if sharing a private joke. "He was in the younger group, of course. Howard was an instructor. He races now. Perhaps you've heard of him?"

Melissa cocked her head to the side as if considering it. "Hmm. Howard Fendle? Can't say that I have." She smiled kindly. "But I don't really follow—what is it? Sailboat racing?"

Howard grunted. "Yacht racing. We won the Louis Vuitton Cup in 2000."

Melissa kept her face blank. "Oh, of course. Very impressive."

There was a moment of uncomfortable silence. Garth did not appear inclined to speak. Yolanda shifted uneasily from one bow-adorned shoe to the next.

"Sorry we can't stay and chat," Melissa said. "We were just getting settled in."

"I guess you were." Howard gave Garth a nudge. "Heh, heh."

Garth's jaw tightened. "Thanks for stopping by."

"Do you have plans for dinner?" Yolanda asked. "I'm sure there are lots of people who'd love to meet Melissa and wish you well."

"I'm afraid we're only here for tonight," Garth replied. "Perhaps next time."

"Of course." Disappointment flashed across Yolanda's face, but she masked it with a lipstick smile. "You give us a call before you come and I'll get it all set up."

Garth remained impassive. "I wouldn't miss it for the world."

...

Garth watched Howard and Yolanda disappear down the street. Old, repressed emotions washed over him, stunning in both age and power.

Calm down. Slow breath. Assume the mask. Don't let them see you get angry.

"They seemed like a nice couple."

Melissa's voice jerked him from his mantra. She spoke with a sarcastic lilt that took him a moment to appreciate, but had the oddest effect of washing away the dark memories that had bubbled so quickly to the surface.

"That guy," he said calmly, "is an asshole. He started bullying me when I was eight. When I was nine, Nan signed me up for sailing lessons. I capsized my first time out. Howard left me to flail around in the water until I was half-drowned and terrified. He said he wanted to show everyone how well our lifejackets worked."

"Why doesn't that surprise me?" Melissa shook her head

at the pink-shirted figure disappearing around a corner. "It must infuriate him to know how successful you are."

Garth paused. "I'd never really thought about it that way." Howard had inherited a pile of money when his father died, but he'd never really made any himself. He was a middling lawyer, and there were rumors he'd lost much of his fortune during the most recent stock market crash. Even his yacht team hadn't managed to win a major event since their victory in 2000.

Garth realized with a start that he was still holding Melissa around the waist. The moment before they'd been interrupted by the Fendles came crashing back.

Heat. Need. Passion spilling over, becoming something deeper.

Her nipples pressed against his palm. The image of her naked, in his bed.

"Um, Melissa…" He had no idea what to say. Absolutely none. Because part of him wanted more than anything to continue where they'd left off, while the other part of him knew that doing so would be an unmitigated disaster.

He'd already acted like an idiot with her. Riding a seesaw. Making jokes. Confiding things about his family he'd never said out loud. She'd seen his home and his dogs, spent time with Jess and Nan, the only two people in the world he cared about. Being with her felt like tumbling down a steep hill, and every day this week he'd been gaining momentum. With a smile and a laugh she'd eroded walls that had taken him years to build.

He hadn't wanted to come to Seesaw. He'd been dreading it, actually, wondering what it would be like to be here without Nan. Imagining the times to come when she wouldn't be here. If it hadn't been for Melissa, he might have simply turned back around and gone back home. But she'd smiled and laughed, teased him into playing like a child. And then she'd fallen into his arms and he'd looked down at her and felt her hands pressed against his chest and a voice in his head had begun screaming at him to kiss her.

He didn't want this. He couldn't do this.

She turned to face him. "Don't say, it, okay?" She stood up on her tiptoes and kissed him quickly on the cheek. "Let's just unpack."

She danced off to the car. Garth followed, forcing his eyes not to linger on the curve of her bottom.

They'd talk about it later.

Much later.

Chapter Twelve

Melissa set down her empty wine glass with a satisfied sigh. Garth moved to refill it, but she waved him off. "I think I've had enough," she said, fanning her cheeks, which were rosy from the combination of the wine, the wood fire, and Garth's proximity. "Anyway, tell me one more time—why exactly did you learn to speak Klingon?"

They'd spent the afternoon in the house, sitting beside the fire and reading. Garth opened a bottle of wine before he started cooking dinner, and by the time they sat down to a meal of steak and salad, the bottle was empty and they'd opened a second. Melissa had the feeling that Garth didn't want to talk about anything personal, so she steered the conversation toward movies, music, and books they loved, finding more common ground than she would have expected. But it was the revelation that he was a Trekkie that really got to her.

He eyed her solemnly. "When you go to the conventions, sometimes English just isn't enough."

She choked on a peal of laughter. "Please tell me you've never dressed up like Spock."

"That's *Mr.* Spock to you, and if I told you, I'd have to kill you. So you'll never hear it from my lips. At least, not in this universe."

His eyes twinkled, and Melissa giggled again. How could she have ever thought him humorless? He didn't share his humor widely, she realized, but it was there, droll and restrained, just below the surface.

After dinner, Garth left to run a mysterious errand, leaving Melissa to sit in front of a crackling fire by herself, watching the red and orange flames dance across the dry wood. She tucked her feet under her and wrapped her palms around a mug of hot tea.

Don't get too comfortable, missy. On a scale of "highly unlikely" to "not in a million years," coming back here rates a solid "when pigs fly."

But she *was* comfortable. By some unspoken agreement, they'd carried on all evening as if the moment in the backyard had never happened. Melissa had the uneasy feeling Garth regretted the whole thing, and she didn't want to delve too deeply into her own intense reaction to his touch. Thinking about the night ahead and sleeping just a few feet away from him gave her goose bumps, so she decided to ignore that as well.

Perhaps not the most mature approach, but sometimes maturity was overrated.

The inside of Seesaw was a far cry from the mansion in Scarsdale. Garth said that Nan refused to let him update the house, so the furniture was circa 1950, the stairs creaked loud enough to be heard across town, and the kitchen linoleum was an interesting shade of puce. But all that only made Melissa like it more. For her, the value of a home couldn't be found in the price of the furnishings or the art; it lay in the memories stored there.

She could see herself as part of a family tucked beneath the eaves of this old house, with a handful of children running up and down the squeaky steps. She could picture her brothers and Tori in the kitchen, and Nan sitting in her old easy chair, smiling her infectious smile.

She could even picture Nan's little white dogs, barking and nipping at the heels of the kids, and Garth playing on the seesaw out back with the kids.

When she pictured him smiling and laughing, she knew she had drifted into a complete fantasy world.

Enough already. Don't just sit here daydreaming about nonsense. Read a book—write an email—do anything that will get your mind off kids.

And husbands.

And families.

"Gah!" Melissa set her cup down on the side table beside her chair. "Enough already!" she said. "If and when you get in another relationship, it's going to be with an easy-going, open, loving guy who will worship the ground you walk on."

Which is to say, absolutely not *Garth Solen.*

She stood and stretched, then got her coat from the closet and put it on. Sitting around never did anyone good. A walk would surely help her state of mind.

Crisp, cold air and a sky full of stars greeted her when she stepped into the dark backyard. The smell of wood smoke and autumn leaves mixed with the snap of impending winter, and her breath formed a cloud around her. The serene quiet eased her mind.

For the first time it occurred to her that perhaps after this engagement charade had come to an end, she should move again. Leave New York completely. Start fresh somewhere, maybe in a small town miles away from her parents and brothers. She'd never lived outside of a big city before, but

Essex had her entranced with its open spaces and quiet nights.

She turned around as the crunch of gravel indicated Garth's arrival.

You'll be calm and collected with him. Give no sign that you were fantasizing about taking over his family home.

He got out of the car carrying a small white box and a paper bag. He started toward the house without looking in her direction, and she realized must be hidden in the dark.

"You didn't bring me dessert, did you?" she called, determined to sound as relaxed and composed as humanly possible. "Because that would be an exceptionally good move on your part."

"Melissa?" He spun around. "What are you doing out here?"

"Just enjoying the air," she replied. "What's in the box?"

He moved the package behind his back. "It's a surprise. Can you give me five minutes before you come in so I can get it all set up?"

She nodded, intrigued. "Okay, but my toes are getting cold. Five minutes is all you get."

...

Garth closed the door behind him and headed for the dining room. He kept reminding himself that this was all for Nan's benefit, but it didn't seem to matter. He still wondered if Melissa would like the tiny truffle cake he'd picked out from the one of the restaurants in town, and he worried that he should have gotten champagne instead of red wine, even though the chef assured him that the Cabernet Sauvignon he'd picked was a far better choice to accompany the dark chocolate.

Quickly, he pulled the candles from the bag and opened

the wine bottle. He set the cake on a china plate, poured two glasses of wine, and arranged a handful of candles in the center of the table. Then he lit the candles and turned off all the lights in the house.

Jess had told him to do that. God knows he didn't have a clue how to set up a "romantic" scene. When he dated, he relied on five-star hotels and expensive restaurants to set the mood. He'd *never* known what women wanted.

"Can I come in?" Melissa called at the door.

"Just a second," he yelled back. Quickly, he felt his back pocket to make sure he still had the tiny ring box, and then turned his phone to the camera setting and set it down on the kitchen counter. Later, he'd have to take some pictures. But he had the feeling peering at her through a camera as she walked into the room had the potential to ruin the moment.

Why he *cared* about the moment was entirely another matter. One he refused to examine. He was doing this for Nan. She would expect a good story with lots of details, and despite the inauspicious start to their engagement, he believed Melissa when she said lying wasn't one of her strengths.

That's why he was doing this. After she'd eaten her cake, drunk her wine, and accepted his ring—again—they'd be off to bed. In separate rooms.

Really.

"Okay, you can come in," he called.

"It's awfully dark," she said. "Can I turn on a light?"

"Nope." He ran his hands over his hair. "It's brighter around the corner. You'll be fine."

"I didn't sign a waiver before I came out here," she warned him, humor softening her threat. "If I trip, I'm suing you for all you're worth."

Her shadow appeared at the back of the room. She emerged into the candlelight slowly, waving her hands in front of her like she was blind. A smile creased her lips. Her hair was loose around her shoulders.

Garth felt a tug in his groin. He was in a house, alone, with a woman who set his every nerve on fire. His fingertips recalled the smooth heat of her slim waist, now hidden by her bulky sweater. His lips remembered the moist caress of her mouth and darting touch of her tongue. Worst of all, his hands ached for the small breasts that he knew were perfectly rounded, with sharp, responsive peaks.

But whatever his body wanted, his mind knew better. So she already seemed to understand him better than any woman he'd met. That didn't matter. An affair with her would still be astonishingly ill-advised. She was already wearing his ring. Sleeping with her could only send the wrong signal. Because he didn't do relationships, and—God forbid—he *definitely* didn't do marriage.

If relationships brought a sprinkling of expectations, marriage would bring a veritable avalanche of desires. Women demanded conversation, sweet words, and understanding of their moods. They expected their husbands to go to family gatherings and tolerate annoying mothers-in-law. They became hurt and angry when they didn't get an anniversary card.

He shuddered. *Not even for Nan.*

When Melissa saw the table, her mouth fell open. "Oh," she breathed, "how lovely!"

At the sight of her cheeks, rosy from the cold, and the sparkle of delight in her eyes, the knot of tension in his shoulders unraveled, and his dark thoughts fell away. "Have a seat," he said. "We're just getting started."

. . .

"That cake was incredible." Melissa sighed and set down her glass, then trailed her finger across the white plate, getting the last bit of frosting on her finger and licking it clean.

"I agree." Garth cleared his throat. "Lausanne Dreams lives up to its reputation."

She took another sip of wine, though her mind was already spinning from the dark, rich Cabernet. Garth fidgeted in his chair. Melissa couldn't help but think that he looked nervous, though that made no sense at all. Garth Solen didn't *do* nervous. Everyone knew that.

"So..." She glanced around, unsure what to do next. Her body knew what it wanted to do—that didn't take much guesswork. But did he feel the same? She'd learned there was much more to Garth than met the eye, but one thing hadn't changed: he didn't wear his emotions on his sleeve.

And yet...sometimes she caught him staring at her lips... or lower. They kept bumping hands at the table, and getting caught in those awkward, quiet moments where it felt like a deep, soul-wrenching kiss was just inches away.

"I guess it's getting late. Should we put another log on the fire, or were you going to turn in?" She realized with annoyance that the wine—which she had hoped would bring a dulling of her senses, and perhaps even some relief from the relentless throbbing between he legs—wasn't working. If anything, it only heightened the delicious fog of a night filled with the perfect dessert and a ridiculously romantic scene.

She wanted to touch him. Damn it, she *needed* to touch him. To run her fingers down his back and slip her hands under the waistband of his pants. To feel hard, masculine muscles and run her fingers through the hair on his chest. To bring back the heady, overwhelming passion she'd tasted when they'd first arrived.

"Wait." He stood abruptly, his chair scraping the wooden

floor. "There's one more thing I need to do."

She looked up at him. "Okaaay," she said slowly.

Garth lowered himself onto one knee. He pulled out a small box from his back pocket and opened it. He popped it open and held it out toward her. "I know this is sort of ridiculous, but Nan thought it was important, and this is for her benefit, so I'm doing exactly what she wants."

Melissa stared at the tiny ring in the box, and then glanced at Garth's strangely serious expression. A diamond the size of a pinhead glittered on a thin gold band. She grinned. "*Two* rings? Oh boy, Nan is one amazing woman. If I ever really do get married, I'm having her plan the entire thing."

The joke cut through the air of tension that had filled the room. Garth pulled the ring from the box. "Just give me your hand, woman," he said, humor mixed with exasperation. "You're ruining the moment."

She held out her right hand and waved it in front of him. "You'll have to do with this one. The other is already taken." Her heart raced as Garth—for the second time in a week—slid a ring on her third finger.

He studied her hand and made a sound of satisfaction. "Perfect."

Melissa stood, and then reached down to pull him to his feet. "No more marriage proposals, all right? A girl can only stand so much."

Garth cleared his throat. He stood only a few feet from her. Melissa swayed toward him, unable to resist her body's command.

He wants you. You want him. Don't let this slip away.

"You know, uh, that this isn't, ah…" He stumbled over his words.

"Real?" she said with a laugh, firmly squelching the nerves that threatened to send her running up the stairs. Her inhibitions fell away the closer she got to Garth's tall frame. "Don't worry. Despite the fact that you've now proposed to me twice, I am fully aware that you have no intention of marrying me."

He cocked his head, looking at her intently. "You're not angry, I hope."

She stopped when their bodies met. She drank in the smell of rich red wine, chocolate, and spicy aftershave. Shivering at her own daring, she placed one hand on his shoulder. "If I'm angry with you, you'll know it."

The candlelight flickered across his face. He yielded no emotions—no softness in his eyes or smile on his lips. Yet she could feel his body yearning toward her, and saw a muscle jump in his cheek.

"What are you doing?" he asked gruffly.

"I'm seducing you," she said, the words tripping from her lips of their own accord. She had lost control somewhere between the rigid muscle under her hand, and the desire that slid, honey-like, through her body. "Just like you were seducing me."

His gaze darkened. "You misunderstood me. I was doing this for Nan."

"Were you?" She trailed her hand down the front of his shirt, stopped at one hip, tugged him an inch closer.

He drew in a breath. "I was. And tomorrow, when we go back to the city, you'll describe everything that just happened, and she'll love it."

"Will I describe this for her, too?" Dizzy with need, Melissa wound her arms around his neck. She leaned into him, ignoring the way his body went rigid when she touched him. She leaned forward and kissed him on the neck. "What about that? Will I tell her about that?"

"I don't want you to get the wrong impression," Garth

said, his voice deep and rough. "This is an arrangement of necessity. Nothing will come of it."

"We're not really getting married, it's all a charade, blah blah blah," Melissa repeated. She kissed him again, this time sending her hands to slide from his waist to his back, lingering at the hard curve of his hip. "Do I need to sign something swearing to that?"

"I don't play games," he warned. "I don't whisper sweet nothings. This isn't what you want."

She looked into his eyes. There was something important in what he was saying, but right now, she couldn't focus long enough to puzzle out the mystery behind his words. "Don't tell me what I want," she said. "I *want* to sleep with you. Is that so hard to believe?"

Garth groaned and dropped his mouth to hers. He claimed her with a rough kiss. "You're trying to kill me, aren't you?"

Melissa jerked his shirt from his pants. With a daring that shocked even her, she tugged it over his head. He pulled it the rest of the way off and threw it on the floor. She sighed with pleasure at the sight of him, his skin tawny in the reflection of the candlelight.

"Depends," she said, her hands busily unbuckling his belt. "Can you take care of business after you're gone?"

"Now that's a question I can truly say I've never been asked." He pushed her hands aside and pulled off her shirt, then deftly unfastened her bra. When the silky garment fell onto the floor, he made a sound that could only be described as a growl, and leaned forward to close his mouth around one sharply peaked nipple.

Melissa sucked in a breath at the sensation. "Never mind," she squeaked. "I want you alive."

He tugged again, and, mesmerized, Melissa found herself slipping out of her jeans, and then her pink bikinis. She had a moment of sudden insecurity when she stood naked before him, and his eyes traveled up and down the length of her body.

She was too thin, too small, too…

"Gorgeous." He stared at her intently, his gaze bringing a wave of heat everywhere it touched. "Absolutely stunning. Just like I knew you would be."

Her nerves fell away. He scooped her against him, and her flesh burned where their bodies made contact. His hands started at her waist, slid up and along her ribs, and finally rested at her breasts.

"Melissa, are you sure you want this? A one-night stand?" Garth's voice was as taut as the muscles that defined his chest and abdomen. "If not, tell me now."

"Damn it, man, am I being too subtle? I'm just coming out of a relationship with a first-class asshole. The last thing I want is to get back into the dating game. Can't we just have sex and call it good?"

He teased her nipples between his thumb and forefingers. "Now that's one female demand I think I can meet."

A moment later, Melissa found herself lying on the soft rug in front of the fireplace. She stared up as Garth removed the rest of his clothes.

"Nicely done," she murmured, as he lowered himself next to her. The entire scenario had her feeling like an actress in a movie. Someone sophisticated and sensual who knew what she wanted and wasn't afraid to go after it.

Someone very different from Melissa Bencher.

"Thank you." With casual strength, Garth pinned her hands over her head. He held her captive while trailing his other hand down the length of her body. His hand came to rest at her mound and covered it, pressing gently with the heel of his hand until she bucked against him. Then he licked a slow circle around her nipple. Even when he let go of her hands, Melissa lay captive to his touch.

He nibbled lightly on one rosy peak and she jerked under him. He moved his thumb and forefinger to the other nipple while he continued to torment the first with his mouth. When he gently pinched, she moaned.

"I don't like to guess," he said softly. "So you'll have to tell me. Do you like that?"

She nodded, though she suspected her body was already telling him everything he needed to know. "Mmmm," she breathed.

"Melissa." His voice was a warning. Swiftly, he closed his mouth over her nipple, using the subtle pressure of his lips and teeth to bring her just to the edge of pain, and then releasing her. "Tell me."

"Oh yes!" she cried. "Yes!"

He licked a slow path around the outside of her nipple before closing his teeth around the delicate peak once again. His hand found the other peak, and he pinched her with just enough force to make Melissa catch her breath. "Do you want it soft, or hard?"

Melissa had never, *ever* been asked such a thing before, and it felt wicked and sexy and thrilling to think about her answer. She swallowed her fear. Tonight, she would try things Garth's way. Honest. Spoken.

"Hard." Her voice came in a soft, breathy whisper. "Pinch me like that. Just like that."

He complied, tormenting her with his mouth and fingers, and each time she felt that surge of pleasure mixed with a hint of pain, she danced closer to ecstasy. He waited until she was mewling and arching beneath him before he slid one finger between her nether lips. He trailed a path along her clitoris, repeatedly rubbing against the tiny nub with a butterfly caress. Then he moved lower.

"How about this?" he asked. He drew his finger back to tease the soft flesh, and then pushed slowly inside her.

Melissa's head flipped back and forth as the need within her body rose. She wasn't sure she'd ever felt so wild and abandoned. "Yes," she whispered. With a boldness she barely knew she had, she placed his hand right over the center of her need. "Right there. Touch me there."

When she balanced right on the edge of fulfillment and knew whatever small amount of control she was exerting was almost gone, she forced her honeyed limbs to reach out and pull him on top of her. "I want you," she said, unable to think clearly, let alone speak. "With me. Inside of me."

She watched in a daze as he reached over to his discarded pants and withdrew a small foil package from his wallet. After slipping on the condom, he rested his body between her legs. He looked down into her eyes then, and kissed her on the lips. He held his body above hers, the hard edges of his hips and groin pinning her in place.

"You'll come with me," he ordered, and it seemed like the most natural thing in the world to obey him. To let her body soar as he slowly filled her with his length and began to move. A slow thrust in and then out, he rubbed his body along the length of her and then entered her again. Melissa cried out.

Her legs rose of their own accord and locked around him. He moved inside of her, faster now, and her body's driving need took over. Melissa gave up control, forgot about waiting or timing, and surrendered to desire.

She exploded with perfect pleasure, dimly aware when he did the same a moment later. Shuddering, she held Garth tightly around the shoulders, riding along with him as they touched paradise.

Chapter Thirteen

The next morning, clad in an oversized T-shirt and light flannel pajama pants, Melissa wandered into the living room, squinting in the morning sun. She'd been disappointed to find Garth gone when she woke up, but also relieved to have the chance to brush her teeth and her hair before she saw him again.

No reason to be nervous. You just had sex—people do it all the time.

Despite her internal warning, her heart still skipped when she saw him sitting in his favorite chair, busily typing on his laptop. He had a dark shadow on his jaw and his hair was tousled with sleep. She waited for him to say something, but he did not, so she kept walking into the kitchen.

Don't be offended. He's finishing up an email.

But she couldn't help but be irritated a moment later, when she realized there was only a splash of coffee left in the pot, not nearly enough for her to have an entire cup.

"Typical man," she muttered.

Melissa started a fresh pot of coffee. The kitchen window looked out onto the backyard, and she stared at the white-frosted tips on the individual blades of grass while the coffee burbled into the pot.

Nothing changed last night. You didn't fall in love, and neither did he.

But couldn't he at least wave at her when she entered the room?

She pulled the loaf of bread they'd bought the day before from its paper bag and then rifled through the drawers until she found a serrated knife.

Sure, he turned you into a quivering mass of jelly, and then did it again halfway through the night. Whatever. You were sex-starved. He probably isn't as good as you imagined.

No one is.

She realized she was waiting for him to come in the room and acknowledge her. But that was stupid. She was acting like the same, silly girl who'd fallen for Mark Venshiner.

Not this time.

She pulled the half-carton of eggs they'd bought the day before from the fridge and rinsed an old cast-iron skillet. She added a pad of butter and set the skillet on the electric stove, waiting for it to grow hot, becoming more determined with every passing second to ignore Garth just as squarely as he was ignoring her.

They'd had a one-night stand, she reminded herself. They were not on their way to a glorious affair, no matter how it might have felt. No matter that, after making love downstairs, they'd taken a slow, hot shower together, and then ended up tangled in each other's arms in Garth's bed. After waking her at two in the morning for a second round, Garth had passed out while Melissa stared at his sleeping form, mystified that so much passion could lurk inside such a quiet, controlled man. Still, there had been no exchange of tender words and no false promises. Melissa didn't expect there to be. He had been perfectly clear about what would follow and she'd jumped in bed with him willingly.

Hell, she'd encouraged it.

But he had pulled her against him, spoon fashion, as they fell asleep. And the arm that had fallen across her seemed so...*possessive*. It was hard to believe the entire encounter truly meant nothing to him.

The butter began to sizzle, and she added two eggs. While the eggs cooked, she put a slice of bread into a stainless steel toaster on the counter.

A few minutes later, she put the finishing touches on a beautiful breakfast for one and walked out of the kitchen. She did not acknowledge Garth as she sat down at the dining room table.

He might have taken her coffee, but she was damned if she was cooking for him, too.

He looked up from his computer as her fork clinked on the plate. "Breakfast time?" he said.

She took a slow sip of her rich, sweet coffee. "It is for me," she replied.

Garth wandered into the kitchen and emerged with a slightly confused look. "Is there another plate somewhere?"

"No."

He stared at her for a second and then blinked. "I see."

She turned away and stared out the window.

See? Two can play the cold-shoulder game.

"I probably should swing through downtown today," he said. "Nan wants me to say hello to some people."

"Whatever. You're the boss."

He paused. "I take it you're mad?"

"What makes you think that?" She felt his eyes boring into her back, but refused to look away from the window.

"Lucky guess." He sighed audibly. "This is about last

night, isn't it? You're regretting it."

"I wasn't regretting it. Until now."

"I told you that this was never going to go anywhere. I thought you understood that."

"I did," she snapped, unable to stop herself from spinning around on her chair. "I did understand that. I *didn't* understand ignoring my presence and treating me like a servant was part of the bargain."

Garth's mouth dropped open. "What are you taking about?"

"You took all the coffee," she accused.

He looked confused. "You're mad because I drank the coffee? I didn't know when you'd be up. I figured you'd want it freshly made."

She crossed her arms over her chest. "Nice try. I walked by and you didn't even bother to say good morning."

"That's why you're mad?"

"I'm not your maid or your chef. I don't make you coffee and I don't cook you breakfast. And you could at least spare a glance and give me a hello when I walk into the room!"

Garth closed his eyes. A look of pain danced across his face. When he opened his eyes again, he looked cool and controlled. "I got up early to get some work done on the ThinkSpeak proposal for Orelian. I didn't notice you come in. I get absorbed when I'm working and tend to lost track of what's going on around me."

Melissa recalled, with a tiny feeling of alarm, that Garth was notorious around the office for exactly that sort of behavior. As a joke, someone had gotten his assistant an air horn years before, so she could get his attention when he was working on a project.

"You assumed I'd make you breakfast," she said.

"You said you would last night. Because I made dinner."

"Oh." She winced. "Forgot about that."

"This, Melissa," Garth said, "is why I do not enter into relationships. And precisely the reason I suspected last night would be a terrible mistake."

Her eyes jerked up to meet his. "What? What do you mean?"

"I make people angry. I particularly make women angry. I pay attention to the wrong things, and don't notice the important ones."

An uneasy sensation entered Melissa's stomach at his flat, emotionless tone. "Don't be silly. I jumped to conclusions. You might have noticed that I tend to do that. I thought you were regretting last night and I was disappointed. I'm sorry."

Garth rubbed his hands over his face. "No, the fault is clearly mine, and that's my point. I never say the right thing." He started to say something else, but then seemed to decide against it. He thrust his hands into his pockets and turned away. "Let's just forget this and head back to the city."

Melissa stared at his back, her mind spinning as she tried to process everything that Garth had just said. "No," she said. Her voice felt suddenly thick, and she cleared her throat and said it again, more clearly. "We aren't leaving it like that. I messed up, not you." She thought about what he had said the night before, when they were making love.

I don't like to guess.

Something clicked and she blinked rapidly as her picture of Garth reassembled, like a kaleidoscope she'd twisted and then held up to the light.

"Let's rewind," she said. "And I'll go first. I don't regret for a moment what happened last night."

Garth turned back around, slowly. "I'm not sure it matters."

She scowled. "The hell it doesn't. I'm not looking for a

poet, or a mind reader. I'm not even looking for a boyfriend. I'm engaged twice over—I can't take any more men in my life." He didn't laugh, but she saw his shoulders relax, and his hard expression soften. "Last night was great—no, it was amazing. How could I regret that? When you didn't say anything to me this morning, well…I freaked out a little. I guess I sort of expect men to be jerks, after Mark, and I decided to get mad instead of being hurt."

Garth studied her face, as if trying to gauge her sincerity. "I didn't notice you come in. I was trying to get as much work done as I could this morning so we could go back upstairs for a few hours before heading out for the day."

"Upstairs?" Melissa repeated. A mix of relief and desire flooded her skin with warmth.

"I'm not going to dress this up," Garth said. "I don't do relationships. But I had a hell of a time last night, too. And I was hoping we might be able to do it a few more times. Maybe even today."

"Really?" A smile broke across her face, and her heart flipped in her chest.

"Really." He reached out and pulled her to her feet. "But you can't expect any more from me. I will do my best not to be an asshole, but that doesn't mean I'm going to succeed."

"Then I will do my best to demand nothing more from you than mind-bogglingly good sex."

He leaned forward and gave her a long, smoldering kiss. "I think we've got a deal."

Chapter Fourteen

After a brief detour in the sagging bed Garth had used for almost two decades, Melissa cooked breakfast and made a fresh pot of coffee for them to share. Garth mentioned that he loved the ocean, so they decided to visit Hammonasset Beach before they headed back to town.

After the morning's drama, it took some time to rebuild the previous day's sense of comfort, but slowly, as they walked along the sand, with the wind whipping at her face and sending her hair spinning, Garth's wry, subtle humor reemerged. He still did not smile often, but when he did, it was like watching the sun crest over the horizon — a tiny golden glow preceded by a flash of brilliant light.

Though he was not inclined to share much of his own emotional state, Garth proved an excellent listener, subtly drawing Melissa out about her relationship with Mark, her experience as one of the few women in the technology field, and her family. Much to her surprise, she even found herself talking about Brit; the way that she'd always idolized him, and how she worried now about how he'd react when he heard the news about her and Garth.

"He'll probably just add it to the list of the ways I've screwed up," she said, trying to sound lighthearted.

"You know, he's incredibly proud of you," Garth replied, somewhat unexpectedly.

"What are you talking about?"

"Your brother thinks you're a genius. You should have seen the letter he wrote on your behalf."

She froze. "What letter?"

"When he sent me your resume, he included a letter he'd written. You would have thought from reading it that you were Albert Einstein and Marie Curie put together. He even promised to personally guarantee any work you did for me."

"Guarantee?" Her heart sank. "As in, he tried to buy me a job?"

Garth shook his head. "No, it wasn't like that. He just wanted me to know he believed 100 percent in you, and what you were capable of doing."

Melissa kicked at the wet sand as a fist tightened around her throat. She'd known her brother had sent a letter on her behalf, but she'd figured it was just the usual cover letter. It had never occurred to her that he might have tried something more personal.

"Of course I know he's proud of me," she said, forcing out the words.

The hollow feeling in her chest said something different.

Brit worked longer and harder than anyone she'd ever met. His expectations for himself were astronomical. Why would his expectations of her be any less?

She'd left home to live with a man who cheated on her, and in the process lost most of her self-esteem and pride. When she'd come back to New York, Brit had immediately started pushing her to get a job, when she could barely get herself out of bed. And now she might have lost the very job he'd helped her to get.

Was it any wonder she'd doubted the way her older brother looked at her? If she saw herself as a colossal failure, why shouldn't he?

"Brit's a hard act to follow," she said.

"Why in the world would you try to follow him?"

Melissa shrugged. "He's been pretty darned successful in life."

"From what Tori told me, they were both quitting their jobs so they could start over," Garth said. "I'm not sure his life has been so perfect."

She flashed him a look of surprise at the insight. "I guess you're right. I never thought about it that way."

"It's easier to see things from the outside."

"He turned around Excorp. And he did get you to hire me," she pointed out. "Everyone said that would be impossible."

"I hired you on your own merits." Garth quirked one lip in a subtle suggestion of a smile. "Believe it or not, I don't give much weight to the opinion of a business executive regarding his sister's credentials. Besides, even if Brit has been successful in business, you're very different people. Seems to me that trying to follow his path is only going to lead to heartbreak."

A wave came rushing up the sand toward them. Garth grabbed her hand and they ran toward higher ground. Cold white foamy water rushed around her bare feet.

They stopped at the dark line between wet and dry sand. Melissa felt Garth's hand tighten momentarily around hers. "Isn't there anyone you try to emulate?" she asked, as she stared at the blue-gray horizon.

He paused. "I used to measure myself against other people, but I always came up short. Now, I try to figure out what I really want, and measure myself against that."

Melissa tried to imagine what that would feel like. For years, she'd measured her success against her brothers. She'd envied Ross for his marriage, Joe for his passion for his work, and Brit for the way he'd turned around the family business. But were their lives so perfect? Ross's marriage had started crumbling almost as soon as it started. How they'd managed to hold out for eight years was still a mystery to Melissa. Joe loved his work, but struggled with the long hours it demanded. And as Garth had said, Brit had recently decided to scrap it all and start over.

Then she thought about herself at her desk at Solen Labs, working on a problem so complex and fascinating that she lost track of time, and the feeling of satisfaction she got every night when she headed home and knew she was doing something good and important and meaningful.

Maybe starting over was part of life. Maybe every time you started over you got a chance to do things differently. Or better. She pushed down the sliver of fear that she had ruined all of it, and focused on the place she was at right now.

On a beach, wearing the ring of a man who wanted her in the most honest, forthright way she'd ever known.

"That's a crazy idea," she said, leaning over to grab a sand dollar that had washed up in front of her. "Maybe I should give it a try."

...

They spent the afternoon visiting with Nan's friends, all of whom had known Garth from when he was a little boy, and all of whom had at least one funny story to tell about him. For Melissa, a picture began to emerge of a smart, shy boy who spent most of his time alone. A boy everyone wanted to comfort when his parents died, but no one knew quite how.

A boy they loved and were proud of, but weren't sure they entirely understood.

That night, a quiet, restrained Garth made love to her until she begged for release. When they fell asleep, he cradled her in his arms.

She couldn't help but notice he'd never said a word.

...

Sunday morning they had breakfast and cleaned the house before heading back to New York. Melissa suppressed a sigh as they turned down her block, just after noon. It would be good to get back home, but it felt a little like the end of a dream. A deep, important bond had formed between them, but it felt indescribably fragile, and Melissa hated to imagine it falling apart.

She had just prepared herself for a hasty good-bye when Garth swore and stepped on the brakes. She followed his gaze to the end of the street, where a small crowd had formed on the sidewalk.

"What do you suppose—" she trailed off as the group apparently caught sight of Garth's car, and turned en masse in their direction. She caught a glimpse of silver, and the bright flash of a camera, then another.

"Paparazzi," he said grimly.

"You're kidding me." She shook her head in wonder. "No offense, but why would anyone care this much about you?"

"Actually, I think they care this much about you." Garth handed her his phone, which he had just checked a few minutes before. "Look at the text from Jess."

Melissa read the note from Garth's housekeeper in shock. "Be careful when you come back. Press is all over Melissa. Check this link."

She followed the link to a story from the Sunday *Star Herald*. The headline read, "America's Sweetheart: Rescued by Love," and it led off with the now-famous picture of the two of them emerging from Hadrien. Interspersed throughout the article were pictures of Melissa as an adolescent, in high school, and at the opening of Mark's lab, Ven Tech.

She skimmed through the text, feeling more nauseated by the second.

"Lonely childhood...ostracized by peers...jilted by Mark Venshiner...life turned around when she met Garth Solen..." She faked a smile, trying to maintain her composure. "Wow, I had no idea I was such a loser before."

Someone had even dug up one of her middle-school class pictures, revealing a toothpick of a girl with enormous braces, thick glasses swallowing half her face, long hair neatly pulled back behind a shockingly ugly orange hairband that perfectly matched her orange pantsuit.

"My mother loved that outfit," Melissa said, shaking her head. "I can't believe someone gave this to the press."

"I'll get the lawyers on them, but there's not too much I can do." Garth's old, steely look was back. "Now you see why I try keep my life private."

She smacked him on the leg. "Don't even start playing tough guy with me," she said. "I'm through feeling guilty about this situation."

Melissa dug through her purse to find her phone. She hadn't checked it since the morning, knowing her mother would be calling with more questions and hoping to avoid them. Now, as she had feared, there were five missed calls from her parents, and two from each of her brothers. Quickly, she shot off a text that she sent to both Ross and Joe: *Haha—America's sweetheart—pretty cool, huh?* To her mother and father she sent something slightly different: *Just back from weekend at Garth's vacation home—will have to talk tomorrow—tired but happy! Garth says ignore press. :-)*

When she looked up again, she realized that Garth had driven past her townhouse. "Wait, what are you doing?"

"You can't stay there," Garth said.

"Why not?"

"They'll dog your every move," he said. "I know how they work. You'll be photographed coming and going, they'll try to catch sight of you in the windows...I'm not having it. You'll come home with me."

"Did you consider asking me before you made that decision?" Melissa flashed. She was trying not to think about the article, but the sting of being portrayed as a lonely outcast was difficult to ignore. "We may be engaged, but I'm fairly certain that does not give you the right to decide where I sleep at night."

"Don't be ridiculous. I'm not having you go back there."

She glared at his stern, unmoving features. "Garth," she said, wishing she could throw something across the car at him, "I have no clothes and no toiletries...what do you expect me to do, wear your shirts to work?"

"I'll send someone back to get your things."

"I'm not going to stay at your house."

"Of course you are," he said. "I have a gate. I have extra rooms. I have a housekeeper with pepper spray."

"I have an apartment, my own lock, and, oddly enough, my very own pepper spray. I'm not moving."

"Melissa." His voice dropped. Became more patient. Calm, the way one might talk to a lunatic perched on the edge of a building. "What's this all about?"

She crossed her arms over her chest, knowing she was being a little crazy, but unable to stop herself. "We were just talking about success, right? Well, right now, success to me means independence. I've done the overprotective father–brother thing and I'm done with it. Understand?"

"I'm not your brother or your father," he said.

"I know that! You're a bossy fake fiancé. And I'm still not staying at your house. I want to be alone, okay? I just need a little space." She glanced at her phone, where text messages kept appearing.

She felt Garth studying her across the car, and her backbone stiffened.

"How about I walk you up," he suggested, "and we go from there."

...

Garth sheltered Melissa in the crook of his arm as he pushed past the reporters crowded around her front stoop. He wanted to punch them, each and every one, and the need to engage in violence was so strong he found himself clenching and unclenching his fists as he walked. Melissa's mobile, expressive face had locked into a cold mask, and he desperately wanted to bring back the playful, smiling woman she'd been only an hour before. He didn't know what to do or how to fix this, and the feeling of helplessness churned in the pit of his stomach like a dark, painful thing.

She unlocked the outside door and they walked up the three flights of stairs to her apartment. After Saturday morning's disaster, which had made clear once again why he refused to consider a relationship, things had gone remarkably well. Melissa disarmed him with her quicksilver smiles and inability to censor the emotions reflected on her face, and though he doubted her willingness to accept the limits he'd placed, he wanted her too much to question her further. Their bodies fit together so easily, he almost felt like she had become an extension of him. When she told him how to pleasure her—her voice soft, hesitant, then more certain, curling with desire—he wanted to burst with the sound.

Melissa stopped at the door. "You don't have to do this," she said darkly.

"I'm not leaving, so you might as well let me in," he replied. The loss of her smile had settled like an emptiness in his chest. He wasn't about to go anywhere until he knew she was safe. If not emotionally, at least physically.

Melissa turned several locks, and then opened the door. Garth wedged his way in first. He make a quick search of the room, checked behind the faded green loveseat, soft armchair, and Chinese screen that blocked off a work area, and then lowered the shades.

She watched from the couch. "Ever consider that you might be a little paranoid?"

Garth ignored her and headed for the bedroom. He didn't care if he was overreacting. He needed to do something to help, and right now, this was the only thing he could come up with.

Her bed was a mess, strewn with dresses, bras, and even a sheer black nightie. He thought for a moment that a stalker had gotten to her things, but forced himself to take a breath. She was the fiancée of a computer geek, not a rock star.

He examined the things on the bed more closely. The discarded dresses were a variety of styles, two black, one striped, two flowered. How did women tell them apart, anyway? Two black bras, one pink—pink? He liked that.

Deliberately, he picked up the pink bra and swung it around on one finger as he headed back for the living room. He tried for a smile. Humor wasn't his forte, but if it lightened her mood, he was willing to give it a try. "I assume you were the one trying on all these clothes?"

Melissa jumped up to snatch the offending garment from him. "I packed in a hurry," she said, pink flowering on her high cheekbones.

"You tried on three bras and five dresses. That's a hurry?"

"You have no idea what a difference the right undergarment makes," she shot back, the corner of her mouth curling with the barest trace of amusement.

"I hope I never have to," Garth replied, a flood of relief choking him at the sight of that tiny, half-smile.

"So you've checked the apartment," Melissa said, "and completed your protective male duty. Any chance you'll leave me alone now?"

He shook his head. She finally seemed to be relaxing, but he wasn't leaving. Not yet. "There are reporters camped out on your doorstep. I'm not going anywhere."

"Do they have some kind of class in bossiness?" Melissa grumbled. She heaved herself off the sofa and tugged open the door of the refrigerator. "Because you'd definitely get an A."

"Why did you have a black negligee on the bed?" Garth asked, ignoring the insult as he followed her into the kitchen.

"What are you talking about?" Melissa had buried her face in the fridge.

"The little lace number on top of the bras. Were you considering bringing that to Seesaw?"

She moved around a bottle in the door of the fridge. "Maybe."

He took hold of her shoulder and turned her toward him, shutting the door of the tiny freezer behind her. "Melissa Bencher, were you planning to seduce me?"

She swallowed. Her eyes flicked from his lips to his face. "Of course not," she replied.

"That's a lie." He couldn't help it. He had to touch her.

His hands danced up and down her spine, settling on the hem of her shirt and then pulling it up and over her head in one fluid motion. He stared at her pale flesh hungrily. This need he felt was dangerous. He knew that. But he could no more deny it than he could have stopped the waves on the beach. It rolled in him, as relentless and consuming as the tide.

"What would you have said if I had?" Melissa asked.

He motioned toward her bedroom. "Why don't you take a chance and find out?"

She paused, body still, expression suddenly serious. "I should warn you, I'm not feeling particularly fun and flirty right now."

He studied her for a long moment, and her nipples hardened under his gaze. He took one finger and traced the edge of her bra, following the scalloped edge down to the center of her chest and back up the other side. She closed her eyes, and he felt her quiver under his hand. His thumbs slid over the center of her breast.

"I have found," he said softly, "that it is important, when faced with ignorant, asshole reporters, to find some way of distracting one's self."

With a quick motion, he released the back clasp and slid the bra off her shoulders.

She drew in a breath. "Oh really? What sort of distraction would you recommend?"

He tugged on the top of her pants. "Something physical. Preferably something pleasurable."

...

Tingles zipped through Melissa at the warmth of his hands on her stomach. In a few quick, easy motions, Garth had released the top button of her pants, and slid his hands down her hips to the edge of her panties. The nervous tension and sick feeling in the pit of her stomach finally started to ease. Though she had not questioned him when he said there could be nothing more between them than sex, right now the warmth of his attention was like a balm to her soul. She didn't know how, but he seemed to understand exactly what she needed. Pushing him away never even crossed her mind.

"Could you be more specific?" she said, the moment almost too perfect, the pleasure too intense and sudden.

"Put it on for me," he said, as he dipped his mouth to her neck. He trailed a line of kisses from the hollow of her neck to behind her ear. Her nipples formed hard peaks against his chest, and she had to fight to catch her breath. "I want to see your skin under that lace."

Melissa swayed at the rush of desire. She opened her eyes and tried to focus on his face. His dark eyes felt like they could consume her whole. "But…"

He cupped her breast in one hand, dropping his mouth to suck on the firm, pebbled flesh. She gasped. Liquid heat flowed through her body.

"Put it on," he repeated, his voice part whisper, part command.

Wordless, she nodded, and headed for the bedroom. The black negligee lay on the bed, just where she had left it when she was packing. She'd struggled with whether to bring it, knowing it was probably silly to think she'd use it, but hoping that she might just the same.

Now, her head spinning, she pushed aside thoughts of the reporters, "America's Sweetheart," and the awful comments that were certain to follow, and stood at the edge of her bed. Resolutely, she stripped off the rest of her clothes and put on the soft lace garment. She was about to turn around to go back into the living room when she felt a pair of arms close around her from behind.

Warm breath tickled her neck. He must have shed his clothes somewhere between the living room and bedroom, because his erection bumped against her back. Melissa caught her breath as his hands cupped her breasts and then slid down her sides to her hips. He pulled her against him.

"You have no idea how perfect you are," he whispered. "How beautiful."

She arched her back, letting him ride against the cleft of her bottom. He slid his hand down the front of her body, nibbling on her neck as he did. More kisses followed, along the tender flesh behind her ear, on end of each collarbone, at the base of her spine. He thrust his hips lightly against her as he weighed her breasts in his hands. When she moaned, he pushed up the hem of the skirt of the negligee so he could run his hands over her bare flesh.

Gently but firmly, he pressed against her shoulder, and Melissa bent forward, resting on her elbows. Adrenaline and desire raced through her in equal measure. She'd never experimented with positions before, and the unfamiliar pressure of his body against her backside was both thrilling and a little frightening. Mark had preferred sex to be fast and simple—missionary style with a minimum of foreplay. Clearly, Garth was in a different class of lover.

He stroked her with just the tips of his fingers, awakening her skin from calf to thigh, spending extra time at the sensitive spot on the back of her knee. His mouth followed, teasing her from inner thigh to the small of her back. When she tried to turn around he stopped her, pushing lightly on her shoulder to keep her in place. With his other hand, he pulled her hips higher, deeper into his own. Her back arched instinctively and she widened her stance. He leaned forward to cup her breasts, and his erection slid between her thighs.

Jesus. Melissa almost swooned at the feeling, the sensitive flesh between her legs throbbing, even though he hadn't yet touched her directly. She experimented, arching more, sending her breasts deeper into his hands and her bottom harder into his groin. This time he was the one to groan.

He leaned over her, covering her with his body and sliding one hand down, to touch the pulsing center of her pleasure. She jerked at the contact, the pleasure so intense she sucked in a rough breath.

"How is that?" he asked.

She couldn't speak.

"'Lis," he warned, speaking into her ear. "I want an answer. I want you to tell me how you feel."

"Ohhh," she moaned. "Good…great…I don't know. Just don't stop!"

He stroked her again, and she couldn't be shy or insecure—not with her body reacting to him this way, and the answering feeling of his hardness pressed against her. Then he slid his hands up along her hips to cup her breasts, and butted against her backside.

"How about that?"

"Do that again," she forced herself to say. "Harder."

Everywhere he touched her, heat rushed and pooled on her skin, in her stomach, and between her legs. He forced her to connect to her own experience and to make him a part of it as well. At that moment, she felt more deeply connected to him than she ever had to a man.

Mark hadn't really cared what happened to her. Sometimes he'd spent a few extra minutes on her breasts, or place a few kisses in sensitive spots, but never like this, and it had never occurred to her to ask for more.

Or if it had, she would never have felt comfortable enough to ask.

Garth refused to take silence for an answer.

He moved again, shifting his position so the head of his cock slipped between her legs. She moved, arched, and then reached back to guide him lower, to find the warmth and wet that called to be filled.

"Now you're getting greedy," he reproved, and he pulled back, punishing her with a light slap to the bottom. He stepped away, and she nearly sobbed aloud at the loss. Then she heard him rip open the package of a condom. She moaned with relief when his heat returned, and he finally guided himself into her core. She found herself pushing back, adjusting her position naturally until they were fully and completely joined.

He groaned and moved an inch or two, his hands teasing her sensitive flesh. "Are you okay?" he asked. "Tell me."

She moved her hips, working to find the right angle to allow him to enter her even more deeply than before. When he seemed to reach her very core she stopped. "Yes," she whispered. "I want you there. Right there."

Garth needed no further instruction. He began to thrust, holding tightly to her hips, keeping them locked tightly together. She wondered how she had gone all her life without ever feeling this full, this alive and needy. She felt him come first, and the sensation of his body exploding and pulsing took her over the edge, until she collapsed into the bed in boneless, shuddering pleasure.

...

Melissa awoke to the smell of coffee. She blinked and rolled over. A mug sat by the side of the bed, steaming.

"Didn't want to make that mistake again," a deep, masculine voice said. "I may be stupid, but I can be taught."

She squinted at Garth's lean form as he entered the room

from the doorway. Somehow, he had managed to procure a clean set of clothes and had showered and shaved. All before...she looked at the clock...seven a.m.? "You're insane," she said. "And where's my breakfast?"

He rolled his eyes. "Give a woman an inch..." He leaned over her and she expected a kiss but instead got a light slap on the bottom. "You have half an hour to get ready."

"What for?"

"It's Monday morning." He gave an evil grin. "And I'm still the boss. It's time for work, America's sweetheart."

Chapter Fifteen

The week passed in a sensual haze of long, slow nights in Melissa's apartment, and heated, needy encounters everywhere else. Each time a new article was published, Melissa would demand that Garth distract her from it, and distract he did, with delicious frequency and growing intensity. A delighted media produced pictures of them eating together at New York's finest, most discreet restaurants, holding hands as they entered and exited, even stealing a kiss once on the way out of Garth's town car. Everyone seemed to love the idea that a mousy, chess-playing girl could have stolen the heart of the "human computer," and even Melissa's mother and brothers backed off their constant complaints and worries.

Any discussion of the future, of course, was off limits. Natalie Orelian had requested more documents and information about ThinkSpeak, including a term sheet for the investment opportunity, which had Garth in a positively ebullient mood—though his version of ebullience tended toward secret, unexpected kisses and an occasional half-grin.

Melissa surrendered to the charade with her mind firmly closed to what the future held. Garth might be touching the essence of her body, but she was keeping her heart firmly in control. They were playing a part that had only one possible ending, and Melissa knew what the outcome would be. In a week, Nan would have her checkup, Orelian would agree to invest in ThinkSpeak, and Garth would be free to move on with his life.

And so would she.

...

The morning of October 28, Garth woke up with a headache and an intense desire to crawl under Melissa's bed. He pretended to be asleep when she rolled over, kissed him lightly on the cheek, and then got out of bed. He kept his eyes closed until he heard the shower turn on, and then opened them and stared at the ceiling in mute horror.

Brunch. Today. He could no longer pretend it wasn't really happening.

He'd been ignoring the impending event, blocking out the thought of meeting Melissa's parents and brothers. But the days had passed in a whirlwind of heady, irresponsible desire. He'd been acting like a fool, and he knew it was all about to catch up with him.

Melissa's parents, Phoebe and John, met them at the door of their SoHo apartment. Phoebe had long, silvery gray hair that she wore in a braid over one shoulder, and her heart-shaped face and piquant features were reminiscent of her daughter. John was a tall, distinguished man with a dark tan and bright blue eyes. He wore loose black pants with a drawstring waist and a long-sleeved white shirt, looking more like an artist than a retired businessman.

"Come in, come in," Phoebe called, singsong, as she opened the door to the sunny apartment. She moved in a cloud of swirling chiffon skirts and flowery perfume, batting with her foot at a longhaired white cat that was eyeing the hallway with avid interest. "Quick, before Anastasia tries to escape."

Melissa tugged on Garth's hand and he followed her inside. He could feel his blood pressure rising as her parents stood side by side, eyeing him suspiciously.

"Mrs. Bencher, Mr. Bencher, thank you so much for having us." He handed Phoebe the basket Jess had packed for him. It held a bag of freshly ground fair trade coffee, a crystal bowl filled with the most perfect collection of strawberries Garth had ever seen, and a bottle of expensive champagne.

"Oh, please, call me Phoebe." She ignored his offering and swooped toward him with arms extended. Before he could stop her, she had closed her arms around him in a hug.

Garth winced. He hated hugs.

This, he knew, was not a widely shared feeling. From the right person—Melissa, for example—and under the right circumstances—if they were both naked—a good hug could go a long way. But hugs were rarely delivered under such exemplary situations. Instead, the hugs Garth received were generally delivered by the wrong people and at the wrong time. Those hugs were overly emotional, inappropriately familiar, or exaggerated.

Phoebe's hug was no exception. She clung to him for several long heartbeats while he contemplated appropriate responses, and then stepped back, alternatively looking between him and her husband.

John cleared his throat as he, thank goodness, extended his hand for Garth to shake. "And call me John."

"What a lovely basket," Phoebe cooed, finally taking the wicker gift that dangled from Garth's fingers. Holding it in front of her, she laced her arm through Melissa's. "Now, we want to hear all about what you lovebirds have been up to for the past two weeks. You must be absolutely frantic. Melissa keeps telling me she's too busy to talk!"

The apartment had a large, open great room filled with pieces of art and furniture that looked like they'd been collected from extensive overseas travels. Wooden end tables carved in the shapes of a giraffe and elephant flanked a dark red brocade couch, which was covered with a brightly colored, loosely woven blanket. A long scroll decorated with Chinese calligraphy and delicate watercolors decorated the wall above the sofa. A collection of three intricately painted pottery bowls sat in a row on the coffee table, each filled with handmade cloth dolls.

He might have appreciated the display, which was made with a great deal of artistry, if he wasn't completely focused on the horror of the moment. Three hours, possibly more, of socializing. With people he didn't know. Worse, with people he was supposed to entertain. People who were supposed to find him likable and emotionally capable.

Melissa sighed and gestured toward the dolls. "Mom, you know Delia's going to destroy your little display, right?"

"Joe can watch her." Phoebe sniffed. "She will never learn any manners if we always have to put away everything when she visits."

"My mother insists on tempting the children with beautiful things, and then getting annoyed when they throw them all over her house," Melissa said to Garth. She sank down into the sofa and patted the seat beside her. He followed. "When are Ross and Joe getting here, anyway?"

"They said they'd be here any minute," John replied. "They're probably running late."

Garth's blood pressure rose a few points higher when Phoebe positioned herself in a leather chair a few feet away.

She pinned him with a steady gaze. Her light-hearted exterior fell away in a flash.

"So, Garth." She paused, obviously waiting for him to respond. "Tell us."

Without conscious thought, his face slipped into its usual protective mask. He leaned forward politely. "I'm sorry, tell you what?"

Phoebe frowned. "About your plans. What you've been doing since you made your announcement. Everything!"

He gritted his teeth.

Be pleasant! Be charming!

But what to say?

Probably not, "This is all a fraud—I'm screwing your daughter and I have absolutely no plans whatsoever to marry her."

"Let's see. You know my grandmother wanted me to take Melissa to our family home in Essex," he said hastily. "So we spent last weekend there. It was very nice." Was there more he could add? If so, he couldn't imagine what. He forced what he thought was a smile. From the look on Melissa's face, he was fairly certain he hadn't succeeded.

Phoebe leaned forward, obviously waiting for him to continue. When he remained silent, she arched an eyebrow at Melissa. His fiancée squeezed his knee for a moment before filling in the silence.

"I can't tell you how lovely the place is, Mom." She rambled on for a few minutes about Essex and Seesaw. Meanwhile, Phoebe and John continued to stare at Garth. Garth stared back, ticking through his mind all of the places he'd rather be.

On the Titanic, while it was sinking.
In a medieval torture chamber.
Hell.

When Melissa paused between stories, John jumped in, directing his words at Garth. "I suppose I wouldn't be a very good father if I didn't say we were a little concerned about how fast things are going. You've only known each other a few months. Are you sure you're ready for a wedding?"

Melissa drew in a breath. Garth began to sweat. What was he supposed to say to that? How could he possibly convince two obviously suspicious people that this marriage was legitimate—when it so clearly wasn't? This had all been so easy with Nan. After all, she had already been convinced. Playing out the charade with Melissa's parents was a completely different matter.

He shrugged and forced out some words. "Ready as we'll ever be, I suppose."

Melissa blanched. She laughed nervously. "Talk about the king of understatement."

With an amused lilt to her voice, she told them how they'd fallen head over heels in love in a few short weeks, and how both of them knew exactly what they wanted from a relationship. Then she blushed and said something about his kiss and how she knew from the very first time their lips touched that he was The One.

The sound of her voice, so soft and dreamy, sent a shudder through him. He would *swear* she was telling the truth. Except he knew she wasn't. Because she was furious. She had to be. He was ruining everything.

Why do you care? You're just sleeping together. She agreed to the deal. No attachments, no relationship. In a few days, you both walk away and no one gets hurt.

Nan was doing well. He'd talked to her doctor on Friday. He wanted her back into the hospital for a few tests next week, but for now, everything appeared to be on the right track. Nurse Margaret had reported Nan was sleeping better, and her cough was definitely subsiding. As soon as he got the final okay from her doctor, Garth would be able to tell Nan that the wedding had been canceled. She would be disappointed, of course, but she would get over it.

He would find Melissa a new job, and she'd move on with her life.

Everything would go back to the way it had been before. And that was exactly what he wanted.

Wasn't it?

• • •

Melissa knew within five minutes of entering her parents' home that disaster had struck. Garth had gotten progressively quieter and colder as they had driven to SoHo. By the time they arrived he was answering her questions in terse monosyllables and his face could have been carved from ice. The old Garth, the one she'd known from work as the man who didn't smile, was back. And she didn't have a clue what to do with him.

He'd stood like a statue when her mother hugged him, acted like Phoebe's questions were an imposition, and then treated her father's reasonable concern like a trivial annoyance. When her brothers arrived, two minutes later, things went from bad to worse.

Ross, the older of the two, had apparently appointed himself a stand-in for Brit. He'd crossed his considerable biceps over his even more considerable chest and given Garth the coldest stare she'd ever seen.

Garth had frozen him right back. It was like watching the battle of the ice men.

Joe, usually the peacemaker of the family, hadn't been much better. He'd pushed aside his flop of brown hair, squinted through his glasses, and then proceeded to drill Garth about his family, his company, and his feelings for Melissa.

With every passing moment, Garth had gotten stiffer and stiffer. Melissa couldn't even play interference because Joe's wife Felicity had a stomach bug and could barely roll out of bed, let alone come for brunch, and Ross never really disciplined his three children anyway, so Melissa spent the morning playing surrogate parent to four kids under the age of twelve. Every time she turned around, Delia was throwing Phoebe's handmade dolls in every direction and Matt was trying to play soccer with Anastasia the cat's squeaky toy.

Finally, when her parents disappeared to put the finishing touches on brunch, Ross went into the office to set up a video for the kids, and Joe received a phone call from work he had to take, Melissa grabbed Garth's arm and steered him into her parents' bedroom.

"Is there a problem?" Garth asked, raising a dark brow as she closed the door behind them.

"Yes," Melissa hissed, no longer able to suppress her frustration. "You are acting like a first-class jerk!"

He cocked his head, expression barely changing. "Is that right? Well, conveniently, I'm happy to leave. Just give me the signal and I'll be on my way."

"You can't just leave," she said. "They'll never believe in this whole thing if you do that."

"Maybe that doesn't matter." He shrugged. "We don't have to pretend much longer. Perhaps it isn't essential that they believe in our story."

"Garth!" She wanted to shake him in her frustration. "What the hell is wrong with you? You're not being yourself. You're acting like some pretentious stranger."

"You see," he said pleasantly, "that's exactly the problem. You seem to have come under the misconception that you know me. And really, you don't. So let's not make this into something it isn't. We have been engaged for precisely seventeen days. Now I'm being a jerk to your parents. A scenario not unlike what thousands of men and women experience every day, I imagine."

She stopped. Even though his chilly stare, something about his gray eyes seemed vulnerable. "Look, I'm not asking for a lot. All you have to do is—"

"What? All I have to do is what, Melissa?"

"Be nice," she said, fumbling for the right words. Her heart was sinking fast, and she had the same feeling she had that first morning at Seesaw, when she realized she'd made a terrible mistake.

"Smile, tell a joke, slap someone on the back," Garth supplied. "Anything else?"

"You make it sound like I'm being unreasonable," she said, with an increasing air of desperation. "All I'm saying is that walking around like you're at a funeral with people you don't know may not be the best way to ingratiate yourself."

"And obviously, ingratiating myself should be my highest goal for the day."

"They're my *parents*," Melissa said. "All I'm asking is that you make an effort to get to know them."

"Which is entirely reasonable. Unfortunately, as you mentioned, I'm a jerk. Which makes it categorically impossible for me to comply."

She stifled a scream of frustration. "Damn it, stop being so flippant! I know you don't have any interest in getting to know any of them, but I've got to live with these people for the rest of my life. The least you can do is act like there's some reason I might possibly be attracted to you."

"Luckily for you," Garth pointed out, "you don't actually have to marry me. In a few days, Nan gets the final okay to resume normal activities. After that, you dump me and we go on with our lives like nothing ever happened. You can tell your family all about how painful it was to be engaged to the human computer. And then you can laugh about how lucky you were to get away."

His words landed like rocks at the pit of her stomach. "Don't. I'd never do that."

"Nonsense. We're just pretending, remember? None of this matters." He punctuated each word in crisp, clinical relief. "Nan sees Dr. Caldy on Friday. After that, our engagement will be over. You can tell your family you've realized the error of your ways and wouldn't marry me if I paid you a million dollars. That should patch things up, don't you think?"

Fear snaked its way through her heart. Melissa watched as he pulled his phone from his pocket and stared at the screen. She took the device from his hands. "Garth, this has nothing to do with our engagement. This has to do with you. And me. And the people on the other side of this door who have no idea who you really are. I know my parents are a little nuts, and my mom drives me crazy sometimes, but they're still my parents. They love me, and this is hurting them. Can't you see that?"

He met her gaze for just a moment before looking away. "You're asking for something I can't give," he said. "Something I don't have. I'm sorry if it's embarrassing for you."

"I'm not embarrassed," Melissa said. "I just want to understand. No, let me restate that. I *need* to understand. I've spent almost every day over the past two weeks with you and I know you aren't always like this. Is it because they're my parents? Or because my brothers are giving you a hard time?"

"You knew this was coming," Garth said. "I told you—I don't do small talk. I don't do relationships or emotions. No warm and fuzzy. I made all these things clear, but you obviously invented some kind of expectation based on who you thought I was, not who I am." He started to push past her, but she caught his arm.

"Garth." She turned him around. He looked away. She reached up and held his face between her palms. "Talk to me."

"There's nothing more to say."

"That's bullshit. Are you nervous around them? They'd understand, you know."

He started to pull away. "We should go back."

"No." Melissa knew in that moment that she was on the verge of losing him. Of losing everything they'd created. "I'm not letting you disappear like this."

Words wouldn't bring him back. She knew that. But what would?

Desperate, she did the only thing she could think to do. She wound her arms around his neck and kissed him. Hard.

For a moment, he did not respond. He simply stood there, rigid, and she thought she had failed. But then his body melted, and he reached for her and drew her against him, his mouth seeking hungrily against hers. She felt need in his kiss, a need so intense she might have been frightened, had her body not reacted with its own desire.

Aching. Wanting. Something more than sexual.

She wanted to know him.

To understand.

He buried his hands in her hair and tugged, causing the loose knot at the back of her head to fall apart. His fingers grazed her scalp. He was taut and controlled, but she felt the edge of wildness underneath.

"Garth, I…"

He silenced her with a kiss so deep and tender she felt it race all the way through her heart. When she was shuddering, her bones weak and formless, he pulled back to stare into her eyes.

"I can't—" he started to speak but then fell silent.

"You can't what?" she prompted. The mix of power and fragility of the moment was nearly overwhelming, and she had to force the words from her throat, worrying all the while that the mere sound of her voice would scare him away.

"I can't do this," Garth started again, his voice strangled. The words came in jerks, some fast, some slow. "I don't know how to make conversation. I always say the wrong thing. Sometimes I practice jokes ahead of time, so I'll have something to say, but it never works. It always falls flat."

Melissa froze. There was pain, deep and dark, in his words. Pain she hadn't begun to guess was there. "We don't have to stay," she said quickly. "I'll tell them you're not feeling well. Or that I'm not feeling well."

He shook his head. "It's not worth it. You've lied enough. In a few days this will be over and you can put it all behind you."

"What if I don't want to put it behind me?" Her voice quavered and she paused. She didn't know what she was about to say, but she felt herself on the top of the mountain and she hesitated, not yet ready to jump off.

Garth must have felt her fear, because he turned away and said wearily, "You don't want this. It won't work. Trust me, I know. I've tried it before."

"But you know *me*," she said, her voice feeling small and insignificant against the strength of his conviction. "I don't know what's happened before, but I don't care about the small talk or the jokes. None of that matters."

"Of course it does. Look, you're imagining something that isn't there for us. I'm sorry I've upset your family, but—" He started to say something else, but a knock on the door interrupted him.

"Melissa, honey, what's going on?"

It was her father. She did not look away from Garth's steely gaze. "Just a sec, Dad."

"Melissa." The warning in her father's voice was impossible to miss. "Everyone is waiting."

With a few brisk movements, Garth straightened his shirt, and then hers. He tucked a stray piece of hair behind her ear before turning back to the door. The transformation happened so fast, Melissa almost didn't believe what she was seeing.

By the time he reached the threshold his face held no expression. No sign that a moment before he had been kissing her as if their lives depended on it. He opened the door and looked into the face of her father.

"So sorry," he murmured politely. "I had a phone call I needed to take."

The chilly stranger was back.

...

None of this had been a surprise. Still, the pain built, so raw and deep he had to bury it further inside his soul than anything ever he'd buried before. Below Samantha. Below Howard Fendle and a dozen other bullies. He clutched a cup of coffee and stared down Melissa's brother Ross the way he had learned in college.

Reveal nothing. Keep the anger inside. Stay calm.

"Things must be a little awkward around the office," Ross said. "I bet your HR department wasn't happy about it." His words might have been intended vaguely as a joke, but they emerged as more of a threat. "I think I saw a training video just last week about the dangers of dating my employees."

Ross, Garth had just learned, managed a construction

crew of about a hundred. He had thick black hair and, like Melissa, arresting blue eyes. But his eyes—and the large, capable fists at his sides—were distinctly unfriendly.

"Is that right?" Garth replied. "How ironic."

He didn't want to be talking to Ross. He didn't want to talk to John, or even mild-mannered Joe, who looked more bewildered and concerned than angry. But at least talking to them was better than talking to Melissa. He couldn't even look at her. Not now, when he'd just spilled words that burned his throat and left him shaking.

It isn't worth the pain.

Ross was circling him like a wolf, looking for an exposed Achilles heel. "I heard you weren't ready to set a date just yet."

"Nope." Garth put his hands on his pockets and adopted a bored expression. He had the feeling this would infuriate his interrogator, and he was right. Across the room Melissa tried to catch his eye. He ignored her. He'd almost lost it, back there in her parents' bedroom, and he knew he'd now have to work that much harder to re-erect the walls she kept trying to break down.

Ross leaned forward, dropping his voice. "I don't know what your game is, but if you hurt her, I'll see that you pay, understand?"

Garth didn't react, just maintained a chilly distance between them. Finally, Ross made a sound of disgust and walked away.

Garth knew it was time that he did the same.

• • •

They waved good-bye at noon, even though they had planned to stay until one. Melissa got into the car with a feeling of dread. After that intense moment in her parents' bedroom, things had fallen from bad to worse. The conversation had been stilted, the air rife with tension. John had turned on his full protective-father mode. He'd gone so far as to ask that they consider calling off the engagement, at least until they had a little more time to get to know each other. Garth had barely reacted to the suggestion at all.

"I understand your concern, John," he'd said, "but Melissa is an adult. I think you'll have to leave it to her to make that decision."

Phoebe had cornered her in the kitchen, her eyes tearing as she grabbed Melissa's shoulders. "'Lis, honey, this isn't right," she said. "You deserve so much more than this. I don't understand why you're doing this but please, reconsider. Can't you see that you're making a terrible mistake?"

"Mom, I'm not going to do something stupid," Melissa said, her own throat tightening at her mother's concern. "He isn't usually like this. Trust me, I know what I'm doing."

Ross left after they ate, claiming that Matt had an early soccer practice that afternoon. He gave Garth a baleful look that spoke volumes as he walked out the door. Joe disappeared a few minutes later. He said he needed to take care of Felicity. His hug and whispered "Call me if you need anything" nearly broke Melissa's heart.

She didn't know who to worry about more—her parents, her brothers, or her fake fiancé.

Back at her apartment, Garth walked her upstairs, but stopped at the door.

"Don't you want to come in?" Melissa asked. She wanted to say more but the words died in her throat. His expression darkened into a formidable scowl.

"Sorry. I've got a lot to do. I'll probably just head to the office for the rest of the day." He gestured toward the front of the building, with its by-now usual coterie of photographers. "I'll have a driver come pick you up in the morning so you don't have to take the train."

"You aren't coming back," she said.

"No."

She swallowed hard, forcing down the pride that stuck in her throat. "Please," she whispered. "Stay. Talk to me."

He did not pause. "I can't."

Part of her wanted to beg and plead, but she knew with a sickening clarity that he would not change his mind. The walls had gone up, and he had no intention of letting her back inside. "I understand," she said, defeated. "Say hi to Nan and the dogs for me."

"I will."

He paused at the doorway. She waited, hoping he might say something more, but his lips simply tightened. A moment of silence passed between them before he turned around and walked away.

Chapter Sixteen

Garth tossed the remainder of his glass of single-malt whisky down his throat. The expensive liquid created a slow burn in its wake. The sensation was pleasurable, just like the buzzing in his head. He contemplated pouring another drink, but that seemed to require a great deal of effort.

"Don't you think you've had enough?" Jess's voice came from the doorway.

He squinted at her. Granted, she was a little fuzzy, but he hardly thought that meant he couldn't have one more drink. "You are a busybody," he proclaimed. The words slurred a little. He tried to remember how many glasses he had consumed. Two? Three?

Jess frowned. "Wow, you really *are* drunk."

"Maybe." He focused on the half-full bottle of amber liquid. Had it been full when he started drinking? Surely not. Maybe he'd had four drinks, but not more than that.

"I called your fiancée."

Garth straightened abruptly. The glass fell from his hand and landed with a thud on the thick Oriental carpet. Han Solo, who had been curled up in Garth's lap, raised his head accusingly. Garth scratched him behind the ears and the dog settled back down.

"Why," he said, priding himself on the calm sound of his voice, "in the name of all that is holy did you do that?"

"Because you obviously had a fight and you need to work things out."

"We didn't have a fight."

"Right. And you're drinking yourself into a stupor because you're happy about something?"

"What makes you think I'm not happy?"

"Garth," Jess said patiently. "I've never seen you do this before."

"So? Maybe I'm turning over a new leaf. Maybe I've decided to start trying to increase my tolerance to alcohol."

Jess snorted. "Right. And maybe you're going to get rid of your *Star Wars* action figure collection."

Garth leaned over to pick up his glass. "I'm going to pour myself another drink," he said as he stretched out his hand. The damned glass must have had legs, because every time he tried to close his hand around it, the stupid thing slid out of his reach. He leaned forward a few more inches. "Because I'm happy," he continued. "And relaxed. Sometimes happy and relaxed men drink a lot."

"I sent a car for her. They just buzzed from the front gate."

Garth fell out of his chair. Han leaped to safety just in time to avoid being squashed beneath Garth's falling body. "I am on the floor," he announced to Jess a moment later, "because I want to be. Please don't misinterpret what just occurred."

"I wouldn't dream of it."

He blinked a few times. Was Chewbacca in the room now? The single image of a little white dog had turned into two little white dogs. Which seemed odd, because the last time he checked, Chewy and Luke were sleeping with Nan.

A ringing sound started in his ears. He winced and wrapped his hands around his head. "That," he declared, "is very unpleasant."

"She must be at the door. I'll be right back," Jess said. "Don't go anywhere."

This seemed like a patently ridiculous thing for her to say, as his legs had completely stopped working. Garth rolled onto his back and stared at the ceiling. This felt better, but then the room started to spin, so he pushed himself to a sitting position.

"Han," he said, squinting to focus on the dancing outline of the dog that sat a few feet away. "Women are a disaster, do you hear me? A complete and utter disaster. You should be glad you only have your brothers to deal with."

The dog nodded, panting.

"I'm glad you agree." He closed his eyes and tried to remember how he'd gotten on the floor. It must have been Melissa's fault.

Melissa.

Sensitive, emotional Melissa.

He had made some colossal mistake with her, the specifics of which eluded him right now. Perhaps it had simply been in hiring her. Truly, if he hadn't hired her, none of this would have happened.

Maybe he should fire her. Would that solve the problem? He had a bad feeling it would not. Besides, thinking about her going away made him want to drink the rest of the bottle of whisky.

"Garth?"

He looked up. A female form was silhouetted in the doorway. "Jess, I told you to leave me alone."

"Why are you on the floor?"

"I already told you. I am here because I want to be."

"What are you talking about? Are you drunk?"

And she said *he* was drunk? Hadn't he just had this conversation with her?

He put his hands underneath his legs and pushed to his feet. He swayed on the way up, and the woman from the door rushed to his side.

"Hold still," she murmured, tucking her body against his and looping her arm around his waist. "We've got to get you into bed."

He frowned. "Melissa, is that you?"

A bright blue pair of eyes met his.

Damn, she was beautiful.

"Yes," she said, her voice sounding as if it was coming from a distance. "And I'm taking you to bed."

"But you're mad at me," he said.

"I'm not mad at you."

"Yes, you are." He struggled to remember why. "I was mean to your parents. And your brothers hate me."

"They don't understand. This is a very complicated situation."

Not as complicated as moving his legs turned out to be. He stared down at his feet, which seemed to be heading in opposite directions.

"Do you need help, Melissa?"

Now that *was* Jess. He swung around to glare at her. He vaguely remembered that she had made him angry, though he wasn't entirely sure how. Still, he tried to channel some righteous indignation. "Haven't you done enough?"

She held up her hands in surrender. "Fine. I'm headed home. You got him?"

Melissa nodded. "I think so. We can always bed down here in the study if need be."

"Nurse Margaret sleeps in the room next to Nan. If you have any trouble, just give her a ring."

"I do *not* need a nurse," Garth said. He paused to untangle his feet. "I will see you in the morning, Jess."

She saluted him briskly. "Aye, aye, captain. I'm sure it will be a bright and early one for you."

He ignored her. The floor had become uneven, and he needed all his attention to keep from falling down.

Melissa tightened her hold around his waist. "Are you ready to try the stairs?"

"Of course. Why do you ask?"

"Because you're leaning against the wall."

He started, surprised to find that the wall was, indeed, pushing against his shoulder. He righted himself and headed for the stairs. Left foot. Right. Left. He pretended his feet were soldiers and he was ordering them into battle.

Onward, brave soldiers!

"What's so funny?" Melissa asked.

He chuckled. "Ah, it's really a private joke."

She snorted. "I suppose it's good to see you laughing."

"Nan used to call me Mr. Silly Pants," he told her gravely. "When I was younger."

"I hope it wasn't last year," Melissa said. She steered him around a landing and up the next flight of stairs. "I have to admit, I can't imagine you being silly."

Garth pushed back his nose and crossed his eyes. "How's that for silly?"

Melissa laughed. He started to do the same, but the movement cost him his balance and he had to grab the railing to keep from tumbling down the stairs. "Whoa!"

"Whoa is right. Let's keep the jokes to a minimum until you get in bed, Mr. Silly Pants."

Still chuckling, Garth pulled himself up the railing.

"You're cute when you laugh."

"So are you."

They got to the top of the stairs. He turned around and pulled her into his arms. "Cute and sexy." He kissed her deeply. She responded to him for a moment, then pushed at his chest, breaking the contact between them.

"I don't think this is a good idea," she said.

He studied her. She had a small halo around her head, perhaps because of the light behind her, or perhaps because he was squinting hard to keep her from turning into three identical twins.

"What's not a bad idea? Sleeping with me?" he cocked his head, confused. "Haven't you already done that?"

A smile brushed across her face. "Yes, I have. More than once."

He pulled her more tightly into his arms. "Well, then, it's a bit late for second-guessing, isn't it?"

She laughed, and he felt something tug inside his chest. Why couldn't he make her laugh more often? Why did this have to feel so strange and comfortable, all at once?

"You were the one who left me," she said, poking a finger at his chest.

He knit his brows together, trying to imagine what would have caused him to do such a ridiculous thing. He had a vague memory of her brothers, Ross and...somebody or other, glaring at him. And her father and mother, disappointed.

The memory hurt his head, so he pushed it aside. Clearly, it was time to change the subject. "Did you know women are aliens?"

Melissa laughed. "How can you be sure?"

He paused, and then said, with an air of conspiracy, "I figured it out in college."

"I see. Was there any particular woman who led you to

this conclusion?"

That was easy. "Samantha. She was definitely an alien."

"Who was Samantha?"

This question seemed odd. Didn't everyone know Samantha? "My girlfriend. Or I thought she was my girlfriend, but she said I was crazy. I told her I loved her and she laughed. But she kept the necklace. She said the diamond was pretty."

The conversation was making his stomach ache. He didn't want to think about Samantha, or women, or diamonds. In fact, he'd started drinking precisely because he didn't want to think about any of these things. "I think," he declared, "that we should stop talking about this, and get in bed."

"Subtle." Melissa gazed up at him, but she wasn't smiling any longer. This bothered him, so he kissed her, and the sweet taste of her lips eased whatever discomfort he had started to feel. He did it again, running his hands down her body, relishing the feeling of her. He took one of her hands and laced his fingers through hers, bumping against a thick ring band as he did.

She belongs to me.

The voice in his head startled him, and he tried to ignore it and focus on more kissing. More touching. But each time he moved he brushed against that ring, which started a chorus of voices, repeating themselves over and over:

Mine mine mine…

She had a ring on her finger that he'd put there. This seemed to clarify any confusion that might arise. Melissa was his now, and no one could take her away.

"Bed," he whispered.

"Yes." She smiled again, but this time it looked sad. Which was all wrong. But he would make it right.

If he could only get his balance.

•••

Melissa watched as Garth's mouth fell open and he began to snore. She had wrestled him into his bed—no small accomplishment in and of itself—just in time for him to pass out. Now, as the sound of his breathing filled the room, he sprawled on top of the comforter in a position of utter relaxation.

She thought about the pain that must have sent him into that bottle tonight and his discomfort at her parents' house. Then she imagined cruel Samantha, taking his innocent gift and laughing at his naïveté.

And her heart broke right down the middle.

"I guess you showed her," she murmured, gently arranging his hands at his sides and centering the pillow under his head. An incredible home, successful business, his pick of beautiful women to share his bed.

But did it matter, when the damage had already been done?

She thought about the way Garth had tensed when Howard and Yolanda Fendle had approached them at Seesaw. And she vowed that if she ever saw Howard again, she would punch him right in the middle of his smug, self-satisfied face.

When Jess had called earlier that evening, she wasn't entirely sure what to do. She knew Garth hadn't wanted her around tonight—meeting her parents had triggered something dark in him, and he obviously wanted to be alone. But when Jess said he was drinking, and seemed upset, how could she stay away? At least for a little while longer, he was her fiancé. And she wasn't going to let him suffer alone.

Now, feeling like the worst sort of interloper, she stole back downstairs. She grabbed her small bag of clothes and toiletries, which she'd left in the front hall when she first arrived. By the time she returned to Garth's bed, having put on her pajamas and brushed her teeth, he had rolled over onto his side. She debated wrestling him out of his clothes. He still wore a leather belt, and the silver buckle looked like it was cutting into his stomach.

"Great. Now I'm going to feel guilty if I don't get this thing off you." She bit her lip, trying to imagine how she could remove it without waking him. Realizing he was probably deeply asleep, she carefully unbuckled the heavy metal and began pulling the other end through the loops on his pants. When the belt stuck underneath his body, she sighed and pushed against him. Finally, she worked the leather loose and threw it on the floor.

She leaned over to kiss him one last time before going to the spare bedroom down the hall. Unexpectedly, his hand shot out and caught her waist, dragging her down on top of him.

"Don't leave."

He had not even opened his eyes, and within seconds, his breathing had returned to a soft snore. Melissa lay still, captured under his arm. She thought about fighting him, and wrestling loose from his grasp, but only for a moment. Then she sighed and reached for a pillow. She tucked it under her head and snuggled into the curve of his body.

I don't want to leave.
Not ever again.

Chapter Seventeen

Garth cracked open one eye. White light stabbed him with its intensity, and he closed his eye just as quickly. Was it morning already? A quick squint at the clock beside his bed demonstrated that it was, indeed, nine o'clock. Meanwhile, sometime during the night a drummer had taken up residence in his head and even now was assaulting him with a relentless pounding.

Cautiously, he surveyed his body. He was still wearing his dress shirt and pants from the day before. A cup of water sat on his bedside table. Two small white pills lay beside the cup. He checked the tiny letters on the white surface and realized that some kind soul had anticipated his pain and left him some aspirin. He took the pills and drank deeply from the glass, but it did little to erase the feeling that someone had shoved a wad of cotton in his mouth. He felt…hung over.

Hung over?

If he focused hard enough—which, he discovered, was an extremely painful undertaking—he could conjure a vague memory of a bottle of Glenfiddich whisky, his study, and a woman helping him to his bed.

That was it. No idea when he'd started drinking, though the why of it returned a few minutes later.

Melissa. Her parents. Two brothers. The world's worst brunch.

He groaned. Why had he ever agreed to meet them? He should have simply put his foot down and refused. Small social engagements were always a disaster. The pressure of the unexpected hug, the enforced social laughter, and the need to conjure up some sort of playful, entertaining façade was simply too much for him.

He rolled back into the pillow. He must truly be losing his mind, because he thought he smelled a hint of her perfume. He wondered if she'd ever speak to him again.

Hopefully not.

No, scratch that. They needed to keep up the charade for another couple of days. Natalie Orelian had agreed to meet with him on Tuesday morning to discuss investment terms. As soon as the contract was signed, they could call this whole thing off.

Any way you looked at it, he needed to extricate himself from this whole painful situation. As soon as possible.

...

"Are you sure you aren't getting cold, Nan?" Melissa asked. She picked up the small rubber ball Han Solo had deposited at her feet and tossed it into the yard. The tiny dog raced after it. Chewbacca raised his head for just a moment before settling back into Nan's lap with a sigh. Luke sniffed around in the grass a few feet away.

"That nurse put so many blankets on me you'd think I was getting ready to go climb Mt. Everest." Nan wore a thick fleece bathrobe, and had two blankets draped across her lap. Her face looked pale and drawn, and she still coughed more than Melissa would have liked, but a twinkle in her eye and relaxed breathing seemed to signal improving health. "Besides, Chewy is keeping me warm."

Melissa smiled. "No one wants to see you catch a chill."

Nan coughed into the back of her hand. Melissa was relieved that the sound didn't reverberate through her body the way it had when they'd first met.

Han deposited the ball back at her feet and sat down expectantly, his tongue lolling out of his mouth at a jaunty angle.

"How old are your dogs?" Melissa asked. "They seem like puppies."

"Four years old," Nan replied. "And really, they're not mine. They belong to Garth."

Melissa cocked her head. "That's not what I heard. He said you rescued them."

Nan laughed. "I rescued them," she said, dabbing a handkerchief across her mouth. "Garth kept them."

"What do you mean?"

"The puppies were in bad shape when I got involved, but we had any number of offers to give them new homes. Garth turned them all down. Once he gets attached to something, it's hard for him to let go."

"Like with me?" Jessalyn set down a tray that held a bowl of oatmeal, silver coffee pot, and variety of fruits on a table beside Nan's wheelchair. She poured a cup of coffee for Nan, and one for Melissa.

Nan *tsk*ed. "Don't underestimate yourself, Jessalyn."

"When Nan brought me here," Jess said to Melissa, "I was a horrible cook and a worse housekeeper. Garth kept me around because I needed help, not because I was good at my job. Now, at least, I make a damned fine cup of coffee.

But I still burn his casseroles every now and then. Speaking of which, unless you need anything else, I should go see to dinner."

Melissa shook her head. "I'm all set. Thank you, Jess."

"Yes, thank you," Nan said. "I promise to eat all my oatmeal."

Jess gave her a mock glare. "You see that you do, young lady. I'll be back to get your tray in a bit."

Nan waited until Jess had disappeared back into the house before she continued. "Garth doesn't open up easily, but when he does, he cares fiercely." She smiled at Melissa. "But that's not news to you, is it?"

Melissa shook her head, trying to mask the sudden rush of jealousy she felt for three little white dogs and pink-haired housekeeper. "I guess I'm a lucky girl."

"Luck has nothing to do with it," Nan said. "I wasn't sure if he'd ever find someone to unlock that heart of his, but now that I've met you, Melissa, I'm not the least bit surprised he finally did." She reached over and patted Melissa's hand. "You know what a hard time he has opening up to people. Finding a woman he could trust is a blessing I wasn't sure I'd ever see in my lifetime."

"We still have our differences," Melissa said, a shiver of guilt racing through her at Nan's happy tone.

"Of course," Nan said. "He's a proud man, and he doesn't like to admit when he's wrong. You'll learn to work through those things. It just takes time."

Melissa sighed and leaned back in her chair. "How long were you married, Nan?"

"Sixty years."

"What was your husband like?" Melissa asked. "If you don't mind me asking."

"Oh no!" Nan smiled. "Arthur was a lot like Garth. He

worked too hard, and was a bit of a loner. He relied on me to set up all our social engagements. He always said that after he died, he'd wait outside the Gates of Heaven for me, so I could introduce him around."

Melissa grinned. She could see Garth making a joke like that someday. If he ever did get married. "Garth said you spent a lot of time at Seesaw, because you had more of a community there."

Nan stroked Chewy's head. "I did, and I loved my friends in Essex. But the real reason we stayed there was that I didn't think the city was a good place for a child to spend the summer. Whenever school was out I took his mother, and later Garth, to Seesaw. I wanted them outside, playing and swimming. Arthur wanted to be with us, but his job was very demanding. He always came out for the weekends, though, or sometimes even just for the night."

"Were you happy?" Melissa asked. "It sounds like that could have been very lonely."

"I was very lucky to be able to spend that time with my family. It was only hard after Garth's parents died." Her smile fell away. "I tried to arrange for him to have lots of camps and activities while we were there, but after the accident…well, it was a difficult time for both of us."

"I'm sure it took a while to adjust to the loss." Melissa pictured Howard Fendle teasing Garth at his most vulnerable moment in life, and her hands tightened into fists.

"It did. To be honest, I don't know that Garth ever really recovered. He had always been a serious boy, but after the accident, things got so much worse. And nothing that woman suggested even came close to helping him with his…"

"Melissa? What are you doing here?"

She spun around guiltily, wishing desperately for Nan to finish her sentence, but then her heart lurched at the sight of Garth, framed by the patio doors. He wore reflective sunglasses that covered half his face, and his mouth was set in a thin, impatient line.

"Garth, that's no way to speak to your fiancée!" Nan chided.

If anything, the line of his mouth grew even narrower. "I have a headache. Forgive me. I thought I dropped Melissa off at home yesterday. I'm surprised to see her here."

He stalked over to them, radiating annoyance. Even Han seemed intimidated by Garth's dour mood. The small dog approached his master slowly and immediately flopped onto his back in submission.

"I, ah…" Melissa fumbled for an excuse for her presence. She hadn't considered the possibility that Garth would completely forget her arrival last night.

"I called her," Nan supplied, coughing gently behind her hand. "I needed a little company."

Melissa flashed her a surprised look. Did Nan know what had happened the night before? Jess could very well have filled her in this morning, though Melissa wondered if she would have revealed the extent of Garth's inebriation.

"Is that right?" Garth raised an eyebrow over the rim of his glasses. "You just arrived this morning, *dear*? How exactly did you manage that?" He leaned over and pressed a kiss on her cheek. The icy touch made her shiver.

"Don't be such a grump," Nan said, brushing past his question. "I sent a car to pick her up." She fixed him with a piercing stare. For once, Melissa could see how the two were related. "Do you have a problem with that?"

"Of course not," he said after a pause. "It's just a busy week. I'm surprised Melissa wanted to spend all that time in the car for a short visit. Or was she planning to take the day off from work and stay all day?"

Nan's chin jutted out. "We've had a lovely visit already. I assumed you would take her with you into town."

"Fine." Garth's words fell like individual icicles. "I'll be leaving for the office in a few minutes. Melissa, are you ready to go?"

She nodded. Starting the morning driving to work with a pissed-off Garth wasn't high on her to-do list. Then again, she'd lost control of that list long ago.

. . .

As soon as they pulled away from the house, Melissa braced for Garth to interrogate her about when exactly she'd arrived and why she had agreed to stay, but he didn't. She wanted to rip the glasses from his eyes and demand that he talk to her, but by now she knew better than to try to budge him when he had made up his mind about something. So they rode in silence, and Melissa felt tears building up behind her eyes.

With every mile that passed, sitting beside him and feeling his presence became more and more painful. Because the moment she got into the car and looked at the unrelenting line of his jaw, and then at the shimmering aquamarine ring on her finger, she realized she'd done something stupid.

Something dumber than believing her noxious ex-boyfriend when he said he needed to pay an "emergency" visit to his computer lab at eight o'clock on a Friday night.

Something far more dangerous than making up a story about being involved with her notoriously reclusive boss.

She'd fallen for him. She'd fallen for Garth Solen.

They'd spent eighteen days together. He'd slid two different rings on her fingers, made love to her countless times, and gotten down on bended knee once.

The numbers meant nothing. The vulnerability in his eyes

the day before, when he'd told her how he couldn't handle making conversation at brunch, and the aching tenderness in the way he'd pulled her close last night, meant everything.

He had some feeling for her. She didn't doubt that. Meeting her parents had been painful for him, and he'd wanted her with him last night to soothe that hurt. But Garth wasn't like other men she'd known. No, his fear of getting close to people was as exceptional as his intellect. Getting past his defenses would require climbing barbed wire, digging under rock walls, and possibly setting off some dynamite. Then, if by some miracle she got inside, Melissa had little doubt that the door to his heart would be locked, and even he might not know where he'd hidden the key.

With a screech of tires, Garth tore into his parking space under the Solen Labs offices and finally removed his sunglasses. Melissa didn't look him in the eye. Yesterday, he had held her close and kissed her like he never wanted her to leave. This morning, he might have been a contemptuous stranger.

"Don't forget that the Autism Advocates auction is tomorrow," he said, as they waited for the elevator upstairs. "We should arrive together. You can drive back to Scarsdale with me in the afternoon."

She shook her head. "My mother arranged an appointment for me at a wedding dress boutique at three. I don't know exactly when we will be done, but I know I won't have time to travel to Scarsdale. You can just pick me up at my apartment."

He rocked back slightly on his heels, but otherwise did not react. "For your sake, I suggest you do not put down a deposit."

Her temper flared. "Thanks for the tip. Because, you know, I was considering it."

"I'm only trying to be fair. You were getting awfully cozy with Nan this morning and I didn't want you to get any ideas. Just because you found a way into my house doesn't mean you'll find a way to stay there permanently, you know."

The elevator doors opened and he gestured for her to enter. She stomped inside, fists clenched. "If by that you mean that you think I'm using your grandmother in some kind of Machiavellian quest for your hand in marriage, think again."

"Yesterday, I left your place alone," he pointed out. "This morning, I woke to find you in my garden. Forgive me for jumping to conclusions."

"And of course, it never occurred to you that the mighty Garth Solen might have wanted me around while he drank himself into a stupor."

They both froze. Melissa was horrified by her own words. Garth had clearly not expected her to say anything of the kind.

"What are you trying to suggest?" he asked, his words taut with composure. "That I called you?"

"No," she said. "You didn't call me. Forget it."

He shook his head. "How did you know I'd been drinking? Who called you? Was it Nan?" He paused, and Melissa could almost see the puzzle pieces coming together in his head. "Jess called you, didn't she?"

"It doesn't matter. I was worried about you after you left."

Garth swore. "That's a load of crap. What happened last night? I don't remember anything."

The doors opened with a soft ping. Melissa ignored the urgency in Garth's tone and walked into the office lobby. The front desk receptionist, a friendly young woman with white-blonde hair and thick German accent, waved. "Good morning, Mr. Solen. Ms. Bencher."

Garth turned his attention her with an uncanny ease.

"Good morning to you, Bettina. Any calls I should know about?"

Bettina looked down at the desk in front of her. She held out a slip of paper. "Natalie Orelian called. She wants to meet you for lunch. And she'd like for your fiancée to join you, if possible."

Chapter Eighteen

Natalie Orelian was seventy years old and obscenely wealthy. She made no attempt to hide either fact. She wore her white hair in a severe chignon, enormous diamonds sparkled from her ears, and a double strand of pearls hung down over the lapel of her pink Chanel suit. She was also "old-fashioned," as she put it.

Tyrannical, Melissa substituted silently. *Repressed. Judgmental.*

"So, Garth," Natalie said, piercing him with a fierce blue-eyed stare as she set down her menu on the table. "I appreciate all of the materials you've sent me about your product. ThinkSpeak looks like it has enormous potential to change the lives of some severely autistic children. But I'm still concerned that the price of development is going to be so high, no one will be able to afford it."

"That's a valid concern," Garth said smoothly. "But we believe strongly that once we get out of the testing phase, we will be able to commercialize some of the secondary products, which will help keep down the price overall. And with your help, we will be able to market the product to some hospitals and schools, so it can be used to help those children who have the greatest needs."

He rattled off some figures about where the components would be sourced, and how the product would be marketed. Knowing Garth, he probably could have continued ad infinitum, but they were interrupted by the arrival of a waiter wearing black pants and a crisp white shirt.

"Have you all decided on lunch?" the waiter asked.

Garth glanced around the table. "Ladies?"

"I'll have the garden salad," Melissa said. Facing down Garth's stare of cold distaste had left her with a sore head and an upset stomach. She couldn't imagine trying to eat anything heavier.

"That's all?" Garth said, cocking his head in polite concern.

Ever since they'd met Natalie at the restaurant, he'd been a properly attentive, if less than demonstrative, fiancé. Of course, she'd noticed that he steered the conversation away from anything personal, toward topics he was comfortable discussing: autism research, ThinkSpeak, Orelian's previous investments.

Melissa shook her head. "My stomach isn't quite right. I'll keep it light."

"Nothing serious, I hope?" Natalie asked.

"No, I didn't sleep well last night. I'm sure that's it. I'll be fine tomorrow." Of course, she didn't mention that she hadn't been able to sleep because she'd been pressed against Garth's heavy, unconscious body, or that every time she tried to escape from the circle of his arms, he'd somehow sensed it, and held her even tighter.

"I'll have the salmon," Natalie said. "With no capers, and the lemon on the side. And please make sure the pilaf isn't overcooked." She shuddered with distaste. "I abhor soft pilaf."

The waiter nodded. "Anything else to drink with your meal? Perhaps a glass of wine?"

Her frown deepened. "I never drink before dinner."

"My apologies." The waiter made a note on his pad and turned to Garth. "And for you, sir?"

"I'll have the soup and salad."

Melissa noticed that Garth didn't have quite his usual color, either. She supposed that was to be expected, given that he'd consumed half his body weight in whisky last night.

After the waiter retrieved their menus, conversation around the table slowed. Melissa picked up her glass of water to take a sip, and Natalie's eyes focused on her ring.

"May I take a look?" she asked, gesturing toward Melissa's left hand.

"Of course, I love showing it off," Melissa said, forcing a cheerful smile. She held it out for the older woman to examine.

Natalie leaned forward to examine it, her eyes widening. "My goodness, that's beautiful." She looked at Garth. "How did you ever pick this out? It's stunning, and so unique."

"I pick out a piece of jewelry each year for my grandmother for Christmas. She particularly likes antiques, so an associate from Hadrien keeps me informed when he finds something new," Garth said. "He brought this piece to my attention a few months ago, and I admit, I found it absolutely captivating."

"Isn't that right around the time you hired Melissa?" Natalie asked, leaning forward with avid interest.

Garth paused. "I suppose it was. As it is an engagement ring, I knew it wasn't right for my grandmother. Still, I bought it anyway. I had a feeling I would regret it if I let it get away. Then when Melissa was trying on rings, I knew the traditional diamond wasn't right for her. I knew she had to have that ring."

An odd expression crossed his face. He glanced at Melissa for just a moment before looking away.

An unexpected glow spread through her. "I had no idea that's how you came to have that ring," Melissa said. "Had Jess seen it? Is that what she meant that day I met her for the first time?"

"I suppose. I showed her a picture of the ring after I bought it."

"Jess is Garth's housekeeper," Melissa explained to Natalie. "She's a little, uh, eccentric." She gave Garth a tiny smile, partly for Natalie's benefit, partly because the story sent warm shivers up and down her spine. He *could* have simply insisted she wear one of the big, glitzy diamonds. Most men would have assumed that's what she would want, and what the press would want to see. But for some reason he'd insisted on finding something that actually fit her — and picked out the ring she'd come to cherish.

The very thought curled her toes.

No matter that he was behaving like a chilly stranger. No matter that she was unlikely to see him smile at her again, or feel him hold her in his arms. No matter. Right now, she felt the warmth of knowing he *did* feel something for her. Something special.

"Now can you see why I fell in love with him?" she said to Natalie. "I mean, I love the ring, but it's the fact that he knew me well enough to pick it out that really matters. He's not showy, or public with his emotions. I'm sure you've heard that about him. But when he feels things, he feels them deeply. That's the secret of our relationship."

Garth's face assumed a forced smile. She reached across the table toward him. After a brief hesitation, he grabbed her hand over the table and squeezed it gently.

"Anything for you," he said, his voice sounding only a

little strangled.

She assumed he thought she was playing the part for Natalie Orelian.

God help her if he guessed she was being honest.

"You two are just lovely," Natalie declared. "I can't tell you how comforting that is to me. You see, Garth, I believe the passion of a designer matters when selling a product, and I frankly haven't been able to tell if you have that passion. That gave me some concern. I was also worried that your relationship with Melissa was some sort of flash-in-the pan nonsense that would end in scandal, the way it does with so many young people these days."

She paused and tightened her lips. "I am absolutely unyielding in my determination to keep the name Orelian away from any suggestion of impropriety. But I've been watching the two of you in the press, and seeing you together today helps me understand better how strong your relationship truly is." She held out her glass of water in a toast. "Here's to the two of you, and your happy marriage." She paused for dramatic effect, and Melissa held her breath. "And here's to ThinkSpeak, Solen Labs, and a long and happy partnership between us."

Chapter Nineteen

Tuesday afternoon, Melissa left the office after lunch and walked around SoHo before heading to the tiny Estalyn's Big Day boutique run by her mother's old college friend, Estalyn Brokley. Inside, racks of white lace and tulle dresses lined the walls of the small space. A thickly carpeted room in back had just enough room for a raised daïs and a small couch, presumably for the companion of the bride-to-be.

Phoebe was already there when she arrived, arranging dresses on a small rack behind the couch in the fitting room. She hadn't mentioned the horrible brunch since Melissa left on Sunday, a not-insignificant blessing, given the fact that if she had, Melissa might have burst into noisy, gulping tears.

Melissa forced a smile as she approached. "Hi, Mom."

"Darling!" Phoebe threw her arms around Melissa's neck in a tight embrace. She pulled back, narrowing her gaze as she examined Melissa from head to toe. "Are you okay? You look tired. Is everything all right?"

Actually, I haven't slept for two nights and trying on wedding dresses will be an agony. Thanks for asking.

"Sure Mom, everything's fine."

Phoebe turned back to the dresses. "I've picked a few for you to try. Really lovely gowns. I can't wait to see them on you. Of course, you haven't picked a date, but assuming that you can give her at least six months, Estalyn can get any of these ordered and fitted for you."

A few minutes later, Melissa stared at herself in the trifold glass mirror in front of the daïs. An enormous, sequined white dress spread several feet in every direction, including at the bodice, where it was presumably hoping to be filled by a generous C-cup, rather than Melissa's barely B. Thin spaghetti straps did nothing to hide her prominent collarbones, and the bulky bodice made her usually slender arms look like sticks. Stiff lace hung around her hips and fell in a puddle on the floor.

"Geez, Mom, did you want me to look like a malnourished ghost?" Melissa twisted to the left and right, noting with distinct displeasure that her shoulder blades looked like twin arrows. She'd gained back the weight she'd lost during her depression, but she would always have a slight figure. At least now she realized that she needed her clothing to emphasize her slender curves, not overpower her frame.

Phoebe frowned. "We can always have it taken in, you know. This is a designer piece. I don't see why you don't like it. I think it's beautiful."

Melissa reached behind her and groped around for the zipper. "It may be a masterpiece, but it looks like hell on me."

"You're still so thin," Phoebe lamented. "It's stress, isn't it? What's happening with Garth? Have things gotten worse?"

Melissa closed her eyes and gritted her teeth at the unmistakably hopeful note in her mother's voice. "First of all, I'm perfectly healthy. I've been this weight ever since college, Mom. It has nothing to do with Garth. You can blame Grandma for giving me the beanpole gene." Phoebe appeared poised to interrupt, so Melissa raised her hand to stop her. "Second of all, I don't want to hear anything about Garth. I understand he didn't make the best possible impression. He takes a while to get comfortable with new people. Just because you and Dad are social butterflies doesn't mean everyone is."

"But darling—"

"No." Melissa let the dress fall to her feet in a whoosh. She carefully stepped out of the white, frothy blob and gathered it up in her arms. Tulle tickled her nose as she handed the garment to her mother. "No more. I know you don't have a whole lot of faith in me, Mom, but at least let me have the benefit of the doubt on this one."

She felt oddly calm, as if this was a conversation she'd been rehearsing for months, instead of a spontaneous outpouring of frustration and pent-up disappointment.

"What's that supposed to mean?"

"You know what that means. Brit's the only one in this family you've ever really trusted. And on a sliding scale, I'm the bottom of the barrel when it comes to mature decision-making. At least in your mind."

Phoebe looked astonished. "Honey, that simply isn't true. Your father and I think the world of you. I can't believe you would say such a thing."

"Right. You never liked Mark."

Phoebe carefully shook out the dress and handed it to Estalyn, who had appeared in the background, clearly nervous about protecting the delicate garment. "Of course I didn't like Mark. He was a terrible man. Look what he did to you!"

"But you didn't know that at the time," Melissa said, her voice surprisingly even. "You hated him from the first time I told you we were dating."

"And was I wrong?" Phoebe grabbed the next dress on the rack and handed it to her. This one was long-sleeved, with a high neck and long train.

"No, you weren't, but that isn't the point." Melissa stepped into the dress and put her arms in the sleeves. Her mother pulled it closed in back. "The point is that it never occurred to you that it was a decision I should make on my own."

"I love you, Melissa. I'm not going to be silent when I see you making a terrible mistake." Phoebe fastened the pearl buttons at the back of Melissa's neck and peeked over her shoulder. "What do you think about this one?"

Melissa stared into the mirror and winced. "Mom, this dress was made for a woman getting married in Iceland. On an iceberg. I'm sweating just looking at myself." Besides covering every inch of her skin with heavy beading, the dress must have weighed at least thirty pounds. Getting married in it would have been like running a marathon.

Phoebe sniffed. "I think it's beautiful."

Melissa tried to set herself free but couldn't raise her arms over her head. "Let me out of here, would you?"

"Fine." Phoebe removed the dress, her mouth pursed with disapproval. "But I swear, you're just doing this because you want to be obstinate. I specifically picked out these dresses for you."

Melissa turned around and touched Phoebe's hand. In a strange way, she felt like the parent, explaining something to a child. "That's exactly the problem. You *picked* them for me—you didn't *ask* me what I wanted."

Phoebe straightened. Her mouth trembled slightly at the corners. "You hate me."

Melissa sighed. "Oh, please. I'm not really in the mood for drama right now."

"You think I'm a terrible mother."

"I think you're bossy, just like your sons, and that you don't trust me, which isn't that surprising, given that I don't trust myself. Or didn't."

Melissa turned to look at herself in the mirror. She wore only her white, strapless bra and a pair of white lace panties. She touched the line of her ribs, and remembered how she used to hide her body beneath shapeless, baggy clothing. She thought about Mark, and how young she'd been when he first kissed her, and then seduced her in his office. She wondered if he'd told Deanna all the same things he'd said to her—*You're the only one who makes me feel like this—the only one who understands me—the only one I want.*

She put her hands on her waist, turned from one side to the other. Then she turned to Estalyn. "I want something silk. Bias cut. Sleeveless, but not spaghetti straps. Maybe a cowl neck."

Her mother's friend nodded. "Yes. Something that drapes—you have the perfect figure for it." She tapped her chin thoughtfully, and then smiled. "I have just the thing." She hurried off to the other room.

Melissa turned back to her mother. "Now, about Garth."

Phoebe crossed her arms over her chest. "I don't care if it does hurt your feelings. I'm not going to stand aside and watch while you make another terrible mistake. He isn't right for you. I have no idea how you ended up with someone so cold and thoughtless. You deserve much, much more."

Melissa held out her left hand. "See this ring? He picked it for me." She held out the other hand, with its tiny, winking pea of a diamond. "And this one? He picked this one for me, too. And for Nan. The grandmother he loves. Did you know the man you think is cold and thoughtless would put himself through hell to make his grandmother happy? Did you know he was bullied terribly as a child? Did you know how painful it must have been for him to come to brunch the other day, when he hates socializing with strangers—but he did it for me, because you're my parents and he knew it was important?"

She took a deep breath, feeling her blood pounding. "Damn it, I love him—do you understand? It may not be smart or logical, and he will probably break my heart. But I'm still going to love him. And there's nothing you can do to stop me. So this time, you can either support me or lose me, because I'm not going to let you make me question myself any longer."

Chest heaving, Melissa turned to grab her clothing. Her own words rang in her ears. She *did* love him. She loved Garth Solen and in exactly three days, when he got a clean bill of health for Nan, he was going to ask for his ring back. He was going to walk away, and pretend like this entire interlude had never happened.

But that didn't matter one iota.

Love didn't ask permission. It wasn't sensible or logical. It did as it wished, and damn the consequences.

Phoebe stared, her mouth hanging open in shock. "But… but…"

"I'm serious," Melissa warned. "Back off the complaining and the doubting, too. Because once he does break my heart, I'm going to need you."

"Honey, I don't understand—"

"Melissa?" Estalyn had returned, holding a rich, ivory satin gown in front of her. The simple garment had a fitted bodice, sheer cap sleeves, and a plunging neckline.

"Ohhhh." Melissa breathed out slowly. "Oh, it's perfect."

"You'll have to wear pasties," Estalyn warned. "It shows everything underneath. Can't do a bra or undies. I only suggest this dress for women with a perfect body—like yours."

Melissa barely heard her speaking. "Can I try it?"

"Of course. Let me help you."

Melissa moved back in front of the mirror. From that

vantage point, she watched as her mother grabbed the hanger from Estalyn and stomped over.

"No one is helping you but me," Phoebe muttered. "I'm your mother, damn it. And if you want to wear this dress, I'm going to be here to help you put it on." She grabbed Melissa in a quick, fierce hug, and then pushed her back onto the daïs.

Melissa smiled. "Thanks, Mom."

Phoebe grimaced. "Now put your arms up so we can slip this nightgown on you. But leave your bra on. I'm not watching you try on a pasty. Whatever that is."

Chapter Twenty

Melissa was standing in her bedroom, peering into the mirror over her dresser and carefully applying her last coat of lip gloss when the buzzer rang from the outside door to her apartment. She glanced at the clock on her bedside table. Five forty-five. Garth was early.

Damn.

She set down the rose wand and trotted over to the intercom in the living room. She wore a brand-new dress she'd just bought from Estalyn. It had been a bridesmaid gown, but was perfect for the auction. The evening blue gown was cut in a similar style to the wedding dress she'd fallen in love with, but was gathered at the hip in a series of pleats that gave a little extra curve to her figure. She wore it with a pair of strappy golden heels, long earrings, and gold necklace. Her hair hung in loose curls around her neck and shoulders.

Melissa felt beautiful and sophisticated, and knew with an absolute certainty that Garth would do everything in his power to ignore her.

She'd left her mother at the wedding dress boutique just an hour before with a hug and a promise to call the next day.

Amazingly enough, her tough words with Phoebe seemed to have broken down an unspoken barrier that had stood between them for years. Even though her mother didn't like Garth any more than she had before, at least she understood Melissa's choice, and was committed to doing whatever she could to support it.

The anticipation of seeing him after her outpouring of love to her mother had Melissa's palms sweating and her throat clutching shut. She couldn't help but wonder if he would see it in her face. Did "I love you" leave a visible marker on her lips or in her eyes?

"Come on up!" She pushed the front door buzzer without waiting for a response. She hadn't yet decided what her tactic would be for the night. She wanted to talk to him about her feelings but wasn't sure if she could without getting overly emotional. And she had no idea how he would react if she did.

Well, no, that wasn't entirely true. She had a really good idea what he would do. He would shut down. Turn off. Refuse to listen.

But surely there was some way to make him listen. She didn't know how deep his feelings for her went, but she knew he cared about her. She had to find a way to persuade him to take a risk on that emotion.

If only she knew how.

A knock sounded sharply at her door. She checked the keyhole as a matter of habit and sucked in a breath.

It wasn't Garth.

She blinked, took a deep breath, and peered through the hole again.

The vision did not change. Standing on her doorstep was a tall, broad-shouldered man with a bump in his nose and the trademark Bencher blue eyes. And he was scowling hard enough to break glass.

"Brit?" Melissa stepped back from the door, her hand clutching instinctively at her chest. "Oh dear God, no."

"Open the door, Melissa," he ordered calmly.

Melissa actually felt a wave of dizziness pass through her. She sucked down a lungful of air.

No, no, no, no, *NO*.

He would ruin everything.

Orelian. ThinkSpeak.

Reporters.

The auction. Press. Pictures.

She forced her body into action, throwing open the door and grabbing his arm. "So what are you doing here?" she hissed as she dragged him inside.

He shook off her hand. "I want to know what the hell you've been doing. And where I can get my hands on that asshole." He shoved his hands deep into his pockets. That was when Melissa noticed his rumpled button-down shirt and wrinkled khakis, and the line of exhaustion etched around his eyes.

"When did you get back to New York?" she asked.

He glanced at his watch. "Twenty-five minutes ago. Tori's getting us coffee. I told her I needed a few minutes alone with you."

"So you had time to dispose of the body?"

"So I could figure out what could possibly possess you to lie to your entire family, and most of the free world."

His voice had taken on that eerie, quiet quality he only used when he was absolutely furious. "You have no right to talk to me this way." Melissa injected as much confidence as she could into her tone.

"I disagree." Brit ran his fingers through his hair. It had grown long, curling over his ears in a thick black wave.

"You shaved," she realized with a start.

"What?"

"Tori told me you were growing your beard. I wanted to see it."

Brit looked slightly shamefaced. "It was silly. But fun."

Melissa studied him more closely. He looked different, though what exactly had changed was hard to identify. The dark shadow on his jaw was familiar, but the tan on his face, the relaxed attire—the shirt open at the neck, khakis sitting low on his waist—the thick gold band on his finger…

She squealed and grabbed his hand. "Wait, what is this?"

Brit dropped his eyes. "It's…well…"

"It's a wedding band, isn't it?"

He nodded. "Tori and I got married a week ago."

"You eloped?" Her mouth dropped open. "Seriously?"

"You know how Mom is," he said, almost pleading. "And Tori doesn't have any family to worry about. She really wanted you all to be there, but I didn't want to get everyone in a tizzy over it, and we just fell in love with Scotland."

"You are in so much trouble," she breathed happily, thrilled to have the attention turned away from her own failures as a daughter. "Mom is going to kill you!"

"Oh, stop it," he snapped. "We're going to have another ceremony in a few months so she can do her whole crazy Phoebe thing. Besides, you're the one who's apparently faking an entire engagement, which I had to find out because our photographer had apparently been following the story of 'America's Sweetheart Steals the Heart of The Human Computer.' So let's talk about that again, shall we?"

Melissa crossed her arms over her chest. "Let's not. It's my business."

Brit glowered. "You're my sister. It's my business, too."

"Actually, I'm pretty sure that familial tie doesn't give you any right to meddle around in my affairs."

"Really? Even if they're singularly crazy? Even if you've been pressured by some jerk to pretend you're engaged? Even if you're lying to our parents and brothers, all of whom I called before I came, all of whom insisted this whole thing was real?"

Melissa stuck out her chin. "Yes. To all of that. My life. My crazy. Not yours."

"I'm going to kill him."

"You're going to leave," she said, "and then you're going to go home and sleep for the next twelve hours. After you wake up, you will pack, get on a plane and go to Aruba, or St. Croix, or wherever you and Tori want to spend the rest of your honeymoon. In a few days, you will discover that my engagement is over. You will roll over, apply a little more sunscreen to your wife's back, and go back to reading whatever gruesome serial killer novel is popular right now. In a few weeks you'll return and the whole thing will be over."

"If you think I'm going to let him get away with this, you're even loonier than I thought." Brit's hand formed a fist. "Tori told me everything. I don't care if you did start the rumor—he had no right to force you into this."

"He didn't force me. I walked into this of my own accord."

"Right," Brit said, voice dripping with sarcasm. "He's your boss, Melissa. You would have done whatever he told you."

Her blood pressure rose. "Actually, brother dear, I happen to have both a brain and free will. I created this situation and I decided to help fix it. And yes, it might be more than a little strange, but you don't know Garth. He would do anything to protect his grandmother, and now that I've met her, I would, too."

Brit gritted his teeth. "This conversation is getting us nowhere. I'm going to kill him and there's nothing you can do to stop me." He finally seemed to take in her outfit. "Why are you dressed like that, anyway? I've never seen you in that sort of a dress."

"If by that you mean a beautiful, sexy number that makes me look fantastic, you're right. I've never owned a dress like this before. And I'm going to the Autism Advocates auction with Garth. Which is why you are going home, and shutting the blinds, and doing whatever you have to do to keep your big fat mouth shut." She poked him in the chest with her finger. "I realize I've let you push me around in the past, but it's not going to work this time. I'm not going to let you hurt Garth, do you hear me? He's in the middle of a very important deal right now, and I'm not going to have it all blown apart because my brother decided to make a scene."

"I don't understand why you're protecting him," Brit said. "He's been treating you like a fool. You'll never just walk away from this *engagement*." He used finger quotes to demonstrate his disdain for the very word. "This story is going to follow you for the rest of your life. How is he going to repay you for that? I'll tell you—he can't. Which is exactly why I'm going to kill him."

When some men got angry, they got loud. Brit got quiet. Now, his voice dropped to a silky, menacing promise. That, coupled with his bar-room brawl nose, not to mention his fighter's stance, completed the picture of a man prepared to do exactly what he had said.

All of which had the odd, unintended effect of washing away Melissa's anger.

"Of course he can't repay me," she said, placing her hand on her brother's arm. "He doesn't have to."

Brit's bossy, overprotective behavior was painfully familiar. Yet how could she stay mad at him for wanting to come to her rescue? This was *Brit*. The man who had been more like a father than a brother to her. The man who do anything to protect her—even risk a lifetime with the woman of his dreams.

She leaned forward and wrapped her arms around his neck in a hug. "You're a first-class busybody, you know that?"

He paused for a moment before returning the hug. His voice shook a little when she finally pulled away. "I won't let any man hurt you again," he said. "I didn't keep Mark away from you like I should have. I can't let it happen again. Not when you're just starting to recover."

She shook her head. "Brit, I know you're doing this because you love me, but it's not your job to protect my heart. That's *my* job."

The front door buzzer startled both of them. Brit walked over and pushed the intercom. "Tori, is that you?"

"Yes—but why are you answering Melissa's door? Is she alive in there? You promised me you wouldn't kill her. Melissa, I am so sorry! I wanted to call but Brit insisted we jump on a plane the second he found out and he was hell-bent on talking to you in person first. He was so mad that I hadn't told him about this from the start that I agreed but I feel terrible and—"

She started to say something else but Brit pushed the button to unlock the door. He shook his head and leaned into the intercom. "Just come up," he said.

Brit turned to Melissa and heaved a deep sigh. "That woman talks more than any other person on the planet."

Melissa didn't have the heart to be mad at Tori. Not when she knew just how difficult the other woman's road to love had been. Not when her brother's voice spilled over with such obvious affection. "And you love her for it."

"I do." He paused, and a tender look appeared in his eyes. Then gave his head a quick shake and focused again on Melissa. "But 'Lis, I don't understand any of this. Can't you explain, just a little?"

The confused, concerned note in his voice, following the moment in which his love for Tori might as well have been written across his face with a giant permanent marker, turned some internal spigot to "on" and tears welled up in Melissa's eyes. She waved a hand in front of her face and sucked in a breath, trying for calm. "Oh, it's just...the whole thing is absurd, really..." Her throat closed, and she had to stop to hold back a fresh wave of tears.

"Now you're worrying me." Brit touched her shoulder gently. "What's really going on?"

"I'm in love with him, okay?" she burst out. "I love the stupid man more than I can possibly express. So you're going to have to hold off on killing him. At least until I figure out what to do about it."

Brit's reaction—the first wave of realization and pity, and then slow build of anger and fear—hurt almost as much as the confession. She knew what he was thinking: what would happen to her this time? How bad would things get when she was rejected again?

But then she heard the sound of a quiet, feminine exclamation. Melissa turned to the door in horror. The door she'd left unlocked when she dragged Brit inside. The door in which Tori and *Garth* now stood. Tori, barely standing as tall as Garth's shoulder, her curly hair loose and wild around her shoulders, looking happier and more relaxed than Melissa had ever seen—except for the look of shock on her face.

Garth, wearing his tuxedo, looking dark and distinguished, his jaw sharp, eyes steely.

Standing in the doorstep.

Watching.

And listening.

Chapter Twenty-one

They'd heard every word. Of course. Because really, in Melissa's world, things didn't just go wrong. They went horribly wrong. Horribly, spectacularly, fantastically wrong.

She didn't just get cheated on by her boyfriend—she discovered her boyfriend making whoopee on her kitchen table with her only friend for three thousand miles.

She didn't just lash out and make up a stupid rumor that a few people spread—her rumor ended up on the cover of a tabloid read by millions.

And she didn't just fall in love with a normal man—she fell in love with the human computer, and then inadvertently confessed her love to him with her brother and his wife standing alongside.

"Sorry, Melissa," Tori squeaked. "He walked up right as I..." She trailed off, her gaze darting between Garth and Melissa.

She couldn't look away. Garth's dark, fathomless eyes were locked on hers. No emotion, not a trace of sympathy, pity, or love passed across his granite features. Nothing. He was as rigid and cold as a statue. Finally, after an endless, interminable pause, he drew a breath.

They all drew a deep, collective breath.

Garth turned to her brother. "You must be Brit." He stepped forward, hand extended.

Brit crossed his arms over his chest. "I am."

Garth dropped his hand. He eyed Brit calmly. "And you're not happy."

"You used my sister," Brit said, his voice full of silky menace. He rubbed his knuckles lightly, his fist a surprisingly competent reminder that while he might now be a successful businessman, inside he was still the boy who'd grown up on the streets of New York, looking for trouble. "You lied to my parents and my brothers. You're damned lucky you're still standing."

Garth's voice revealed nothing. "I see." He turned to Melissa. "Shall we go?"

Brit narrowed his gaze. "That's it?"

"I'm not going to argue, if that's what you're expecting," Garth replied. "And given that, I'm not sure there's anything else to say."

Brit took a step closer. Up close, the two men were similar in height and build, though Garth had a few inches on Brit, and where Brit practically vibrated with repressed fury, Garth was a chilly emotionless statue. "I want an explanation. I want to know exactly what happened, why, and how you're going to fix it."

"Well, you're not going to get any of that," Melissa said. She grabbed Brit's arm and tugged hard in the direction of the doorway. "You're going to leave. Garth and I need to talk."

Brit crossed his arms over his chest. "I'm staying."

"Oh no, you aren't!" Tori grabbed Brit's other hand, helping Melissa to pull him out of the apartment. She shot a quick, meaningful glance at Garth as she did. "I'm not sure whether to say sorry or punch you, but for now, I'm going with removing my oaf of a husband from Melissa's apartment."

"I'm not going anywhere." Brit's scowl deepened. "Not if he's here."

Melissa pushed him the last of the way out the door. "Sorry, big brother, but you have no role in this." She spared a quick glance at Tori, unable to take in the concern in her friend's big brown eyes. "I'm sorry you had to cut short your honeymoon."

Tori waved a dismissive hand. "I was getting bored of being on vacation anyway." She darted forward and grabbed Melissa in a quick, tight hug. "So sorry, hon. Call me in the morning," she whispered into Melissa's ear.

Melissa nodded, watching as her brother and Tori disappeared down the stairs. Then she took a deep breath and looked back at Garth. "I apologize for my brother."

"It's understandable. I'd probably feel the same way, if you were my sister."

Melissa stepped back inside and closed the door behind her. A chill broke over her skin, and goose bumps danced across her arms and shoulders. "So I guess you heard what I was saying," she said, her voice wobbling. Her heart beat like a hummingbird, whirring in her chest so quickly it was difficult to catch her breath.

A tiny part of her imagined him taking her into his arms, kissing her deeply, and sharing his own, everlasting love. But even that tiny spark of hope sputtered moments later, when he made no move in her direction. If he was going to take her in his arms, he had clearly missed his cue.

"I did." He paused, and the moment hung in the air with deep, painful tension. "But Melissa, you have to know I don't—"

She cut him off, knowing what was coming. "You care

about me, Garth. I know you do. And we're good together. Really good. I know this isn't what you wanted, and it's inconvenient and messy, but that's what life is about." She put her hands on her hips, staring defiantly at him, refusing to look away. "The truth is that I fell in love with you. And you may not feel the same, but at least I know you feel something. So why not give this a chance? Why walk away now, when we have the chance for something more?"

"I don't do relationships. You know that. I've said it over and over."

"You've said a lot of things," she said. "A lot of things that don't make a bit of sense. You love deeply—perhaps more deeply than any man I've ever known. I know relationships aren't easy for you, but that doesn't give you an excuse to walk away from someone you care about."

Garth spread his hands. "Melissa," he said, his voice rough, "you've made up some fantasy of who you think I am, but you're wrong. This is all wrong. You're looking for something I can't give, and you'll only be disappointed when you figure out the truth."

"That's bullshit," Melissa shot back. "You don't have the foggiest idea of what I want, or the man I fell in love with."

"Don't say that."

"It's true," she flared. "You can't tell me not to feel it, or that I don't know who you are. I *do* know. I've seen you at your best and your worst and I'm sorry, but I fell in love with the whole package. The guy who makes me feel beautiful and whole, who asks what I want and listens to my answers, and who couldn't make it through a family brunch without turning into a cold stranger. Why can't you believe that?"

Garth ran his fingers through his hair and turned toward the window. He gave a short, harsh laugh, not looking at her as he began to speak. "You know, Nan sent me to a therapist after my parents died. She worried that I was having trouble making friends, and didn't understand why I got so nervous in social situations. The therapist had a label for me, something neither Nan or I had ever heard of: Asperger's syndrome. She came up with lots of recommendations for helping me adjust, but in the end there wasn't any way to fix it. I'm not normal, Melissa, and I never will be."

Melissa's breath rushed out. She wasn't surprised, really. She knew too much about the autism spectrum not to have recognized it in Garth. Still, it was the last piece of the puzzle, and it completed everything she already knew about him. His devotion to ThinkSpeak. His tireless intellect. His difficulty reading her emotions. She pictured him as a child, his awkwardness and dislike of social situations becoming magnified bit by bit as he was teased and bullied. She pictured him recovering from the loss of his parents even while he struggled to make sense of his own ability to relate to others— or lack thereof. She pictured a boy who was too smart, who liked all the wrong things and didn't understand why people gave him such a hard time for being the person he was.

And fell that much deeper in love.

"Garth," Melissa said softly, "you aren't the only person to struggle with this."

Garth held out his hands in mute acknowledgment of her words. "I'm no kind of partner, Melissa. I'm half a man, and there's no way to fix me. No way to make it better."

"You *are* a whole person. And I fell in love with him." She willed him to understand, to feel what was in her heart. "I don't want to fix you."

A muscle jumped in his cheek. "What happened with your parents wasn't a fluke. Remember how I pissed you off, that morning at Seesaw? That's how I am. I'm better alone. That way no one gets hurt."

Melissa's stomach lurched. "No. You're not better alone, and we've gone way too far to avoid having someone get hurt." She walked over to the window and touched his arm. "What you're talking about is window dressing, Garth. I've seen the person you are underneath all that. I've watched you with Nan, and seen how you care for Jess and those silly dogs. I know what happens when you love something. It isn't what you say to them that matters. It's what you do. It's how you feel. But you have to be willing to take a chance." She drew in a deep breath, steeling herself for the question she had to ask. "I don't know how you feel about me, but if you do love me — even just a little — isn't it worth giving it a try?"

She waited, her breath yearning in her chest, watching his face for some reaction. Some expression. But nothing came.

"I'm sorry," he said finally. "I can't."

The air expelled from her lungs in a whoosh. Jagged, tiny pinpricks of pain attacked her from all sides but she forced herself not to look away. "But why? Why walk away from this before you know what it could be?"

"Let it go." His voice came low. Tense.

"I love you!" she cried. "I can't let it go."

A rough groan emerged from somewhere deep in his gut. "Damn it, Melissa, I'm tired of hurting, okay? I'm tired of trying and failing. I did it, over and over when I was young. I can't tell you how many times I asked a woman out and she looked at me like I was crazy, or the way it felt when I realized I had no idea that Samantha didn't share my feelings for her. I can't do it anymore. Not for you, or anyone else. I'm sure it sounds fun and romantic to try to save me but you'll just be disappointed in the long run, and I'm not prepared to go through it again."

His words cut through her. She hadn't expected that. She had thought he would reject her, tell her he didn't love her, or maybe even look at her with pity. But she hadn't expected the broken look on his face.

"I don't want to save you," she said, low and urgent. "You don't need saving. I know things won't be perfect and we'll fight and I'll misunderstand, and you'll get frustrated. That's okay. It's worth it."

He held up a hand. "No," he said, in a tone that brooked no compromise. "It's not. Not for either of us. You have no idea what it feels like to go through this, Melissa, or you'd agree."

"You think I've never been hurt?" Melissa stared at him, her stomach locking with anger. "You think I've never been humiliated? Or had my heart broken by the man I trusted with my heart and soul?"

Garth looked down at his hands. "I wasn't thinking about that."

"No, you're right. You weren't thinking. You've convinced yourself that because you've got some special label, your pain is different or worse than everyone else's. Well, it isn't. We all fall down, Garth. People hurt us and we trust the wrong people and love the wrong people and then have to pick ourselves up and do it again."

She stared at him for an endless moment, but his eyes only got colder, and his body more rigid. Finally, she blew out a breath in surrender. "Fine. I promised to play this game until Nan's doctor visit, and I will. But come Saturday morning, I'm done."

Chapter Twenty-two

Melissa liked to think she had been through hard times. She had lived through Mark's infidelity. She had lived through months of waking up each morning and wondering why she should bother getting out of bed. She had suffered the humiliation of people looking at her with pity.

She had never felt like this.

Garth's hand rested on her hip. They posed for a reporter and cameraman who were working the massive hotel ballroom with its crush of men in tuxedos and women in sparkling gowns. To the press covering the Autism Advocates event, they were the perfect couple. Garth never left her side as they worked the room. She made conversation with people she knew from Solen Labs, and introduced Garth to people she'd connected with through her own work with the advocacy group. Garth talked about ThinkSpeak, and his plans to revolutionize the treatment for children with severe autism. People asked them, "When's the wedding?" and "Tell us how you two met again?" And of course everyone said, "You look so happy."

Meanwhile, Melissa felt as if she were hovering a few feet

above her body, avoiding the pain only by removing herself from it. She could no more feel that hand on her hip and know this was the last time she'd feel it, than she could look Garth in the eyes and hear him say again, "It's not worth it."

She'd screwed up again. This time, she'd seen it coming. Falling for Garth had been a disaster she'd warned herself against from day one. The loss should have been easier to bear this time. But it wasn't. Nothing could have prepared her for this.

She distracted herself by thinking about her next steps. She'd have to tell her family. The press would find out. Maybe the best thing would be to keep things quiet for a little while as she looked for a new job.

Melissa stumbled as the thought of leaving Solen Labs caught her with unexpected force. Garth caught her under her arm and she had to stifle a sob.

Don't think, don't look at him, don't let him know how much this hurts.

The words became her mantra. She smiled and shook hands. She laughed and stepped out onto the dance floor as if she'd been born to this life. But she couldn't meet his eyes. Not yet.

They danced for an hour. Melissa's head began to pound with the force of her unspent tears. Finally, she pulled him off the floor. "How much longer would you like to stay?" she asked stiffly.

"We can go now," Garth replied. She noticed he had been no more able to meet her eyes than she had his. "I've seen everyone I need to see."

She nodded. Her hold on her composure was razor thin, and as soon as she got home, she would dissolve. If she could only make it that far.

"Melissa?"

She spun around at the familiar voice. "Deanna?" It was indeed her old friend—or rather, ex-friend. She wore her hair in a tall up-do, and her curvy body was on full display in a tight silver dress. Mark followed a few feet behind. "And Mark." She paused, wondering just how much more the universe would choose to pile on her tonight. She waited for the anger and hurt to come, but all she felt when she looked at Mark's carefully trimmed hair and manicured hands was a deep, resounding emptiness. She had no energy left to waste on Mark and Deanna. Not tonight. Not anymore. "How, er, *lovely* to see you both."

Mark looked wary, probably remembering the last time they'd seen each other. "Melissa." He nodded to Garth and extended a hand. "It's been a while. Congratulations on catching her. You're a lucky man."

Garth looked at Mark's hand as though it were something vile. "Yes, I am." He looped his arm tighter around Melissa's waist. "And you're an ass."

Mark's mouth fell open. Deanna sucked in a sharp breath. "Well, I..." She turned to him and snarled, "I told you they wouldn't want to talk to us, you idiot."

He ignored her. "Look, surely we can let bygones be bygones." A note of desperation entered his voice. "It's a small community, you know. Maybe we can find a way to work together in the future."

Garth pursed his lips in distaste. "I would sooner work with a hyena. Everyone knows you're a few steps from bankruptcy, Venshiner. And you've got no one to blame but yourself." Before waiting for a reply, Garth spun Melissa around and headed for the exit. They went only a few feet before he turned back around. "For the record, if you ever talk to her, touch her, or contact her again, you'll regret it for the rest of your life."

Melissa thought she heard the click of a camera and remembered, in a dizzy, vague corner of her brain, that the press were everywhere tonight. She could see the picture on tomorrow's *New York Star Herald*: "Billionaire Solen Slams Failing Entrepreneur Mark Venshiner."

And for the first time that night she didn't have to fake her smile.

Chapter Twenty-three

"So I'm not recommending any marathons, but I certainly think getting out and walking a little bit every day is a good idea." Dr. Caldy fixed Nan with a firm look. "As long as you're careful. Take it easy and give yourself time to build back your strength." He had come to the house for Nan's final check, and now sat beside her bed, leaving Garth to pace in the background. "Just because you've kicked the pneumonia doesn't mean you don't have a long way to go to get your strength back."

With each word, Garth felt his heart tear in two opposite directions. Of course, on one hand he was relieved to know Nan was doing well—as well as she could, given her heart and age. But on the other, he couldn't ignore the obvious consequence of the doctor's proclamation.

The pneumonia was gone. He'd have to tell her about Melissa.

Natalie Orelian had signed the investment agreement on Thursday. She said she'd enjoyed seeing him at the auction with Melissa. He'd been eternally grateful for Melissa's presence, as she'd stayed close by his side all night, smoothing over his usual social deep freeze with her wit and beauty. But every second had been an agony, as he wondered if she could possible have been as calm and unconcerned as she looked. He'd almost punched Mark Venshiner right in the middle of his smarmy face, loosing all his pent-up frustration and disappointment on the horrible little man, but had decided Venshiner's bankruptcy and professional collapse would be its own punishment.

"If you start getting short of breath," Dr. Caldy continued, "or having any kind of chest pain, you need to sit down, take it easy, and call me if it persists. Understand?"

Nan smiled, her eyes crinkling with pleasure. "No aerobics?"

"Maybe in a few weeks."

"I suppose I can handle that."

The doctor left a few minutes later, with a handshake to Garth and a peck on Nan's cheek. He'd been treating her for many years and had become a friend. Garth wouldn't have trusted his recommendation otherwise.

After he'd left, Nan pushed herself to standing. Garth took a step toward her, hand out, but she waved him away. "You heard Dr. Caldy. I get to walk every day. On my own."

"He said you could walk. He never said on your own." Garth grabbed the soft fleece robe that lay on the dresser a few feet away and handed it to her. "I expect you to take me, Nurse Margaret, or Jess out for these daily walks, you know. The last thing we need is for you to take a fall."

"Pish." Nan snorted. "I'm as steady as a rock."

Still, she placed her hand on his forearm as she began to shuffle toward the patio door. She might have been out of the woods, but that didn't mean she wasn't as fragile as a newborn child. All three dogs followed, tearing out ahead when Garth opened the door, and then circling back around to stay close by Nan's feet. At a slow pace, they walked from the bedroom to the veranda overlooking the backyard garden.

Nan sat down on a gliding rocker and arranged her robe over her knees. She coughed lightly as she patted the seat beside her. "Now, why don't you tell me what's been bothering you."

Garth flashed her a look of surprise. "What do you mean?"

Nan chuckled. "I've known you all your life. Do you really think you can hide it from me when you have something you need to say?"

He sank down into the chair. It was time to tell her. But how?

The events of the last few weeks buzzed through his mind. The article. Nan, assuming it was true. The pact with Melissa. The ring. The kiss...

Waking up during the night at Seesaw, and finding her in his arms. Melissa laughing as they walked on the beach. The night of the auction, when she'd been so regal and proud, so beautiful he could hardly bear to look at her.

Her voice, saying, "I love you..."

Nan's soft voice penetrated his reverie. "Why hasn't Melissa been by this week? I called her twice. She said she's been busy at work."

"I suppose that explains it," Garth said hollowly. He wished he could tear his brain out of his head so the memories would stop bombarding him, but they just started coming faster than ever. *Melissa in her office, feet on top of her desk, sipping her coffee as they talked. Melissa in his bed, her skin yielding gently under his fingers, her body opening like a flower.*

Melissa, telling him she was ready to say good-bye.

"I'm not coming back to work. I'll finish up my projects from home," she'd said the night of the auction, when he dropped her back at her house. "You can email me after Nan meets with the doctor. I'll find a new job on my own. I don't want to see you again."

She hadn't shed a single tear. Just raised her chin and stared straight into his eyes.

I don't want to see you again.

That was what he wanted, wasn't it? For this to end smoothly? Simply?

Then why did he want so desperately to do nothing less than turn around and beg her to stay? He'd had to use every ounce of self-control to keep himself from grabbing her and holding her tight. The voice in his head kept saying over and over again that it was for the best, that neither of them needed the pain, but somehow he hadn't managed to avoid the pain after all. Because waking up every morning without her was its own special hell. And instead of getting better, every day it seemed to be getting worse.

"But wouldn't you know if she's busy at work?" Nan asked. "Aren't you the boss?"

Garth shook his head. He gave a short, humorless laugh. "I haven't been Melissa's boss for a long time."

"What's really going on?" Nan asked gently.

Han Solo stood up on his haunches, scratching Garth's knee in an obvious request for attention. Without thinking, Garth picked up the little dog and put it in his lap. "I don't quite know how to say this," he hedged.

That much, at least, was true. He had absolutely no idea how to tell Nan he'd perpetuated the biggest lie of all time.

"Something's gone wrong?"

He nodded.

"Something bad?"

He nodded again. Something caught his throat in a tight grasp, and speaking was suddenly out of the question. He tried clearing his throat but no sound emerged. The thing that had him in its grasp was squeezing now, and the pressure was doing the oddest thing: the backs of his eyes were starting to tingle and burn.

He rubbed a hand over his face, struggling for calm.

"That's what love does to you," Nan said after a moment. "Turns your world upside down and backward."

Garth shook his head. How could he explain to her that wasn't it? This wasn't about love. This was about regret and frustration. And sure, a little bit of sentiment. Even he wasn't immune to that. But love?

He took a deep breath. "Nan...you see..." The words slipped away like minnows, darting though his lips. Meanwhile, the deep strumming of his heart made it feel like the overstressed organ might burst in his chest.

"Melissa and I...I don't think we are going to...she and I..."

"Oh no. Stop right there," Nan interrupted as he trailed off again. "You've got to go after her. That's the only thing for it. You'll mess up from time to time, Garth. Every man does. That's when you pick yourself up by your bootstraps and say you're sorry."

He froze. "No, Nan, that's not it. I mean, yes, I did mess up, but not the way you mean."

She continued, unconcerned by his obvious discomfort. "Garth, I'm not sure you ever appreciated just how alike you and your grandfather were. But sometimes I look at you and it's like I'm looking at an old movie of him."

"Really?"

She smiled. "Really. Like now. You can't imagine how much he struggled to tell me he loved me. Or how close he came to walking away, because he was scared of what might happen if I ever left him."

"Nan, I can't do it." He discarded any hope of trying to tell Nan the truth, and blew out a shaky breath. He'd never mastered a conversation with her in the past, and he certainly wasn't going to start now. "I can't."

She fixed him with a steely eye. "Nonsense. You wake up every morning and imagine her with you, don't you?"

Garth closed his eyes and nodded. "Yes."

"At the end of the day, you want to tell her everything that happens. You know it won't mean anything until you share it with her."

He thought about ThinkSpeak, and the plans they'd made that week, and how he longed to tell Melissa about them, and find out if she thought they were moving too fast or too slow.

I don't want to see you again…

"Yes."

"The thought of loving her is terrifying you because you know how badly it will hurt if you lose her."

He brushed a hand across his eyes, not even bothering to nod, because she was right and she knew it. They both knew it.

Even though he'd only been five years old, he still remembered the pain of waking up and expecting to see his parents, and remembering anew each morning that they were gone. That they were never coming back. And now he couldn't help but think, what if he let himself love her, and then Melissa left him, too? What if she changed her mind or moved on? What if something happened to her like it had to them?

"You learned about pain too early," Nan said, breaking into his thoughts. "It wasn't right for a child to stare in the face of death and try to make sense of it. Shutting things out worked for a while—I understand that. You have challenges some people don't—and gifts they don't, either. Now you've got a chance for something more. Love changes your life,

Garth. It brings terror and joy all in the same breath. And if you think loving Melissa is frightening, just wait until you have a child."

He jerked in his seat. A child?

"But that doesn't mean you run away. Your capacity to love is going to grow and grow until you think you can't love any more—and then you'll love a little bit more." Nan continued her relentless assault, her words etching themselves across his mind even as his stupid, traitorous imagination painted a picture of Melissa, holding their child in her arms. "Everyday, you'll look at the love you've been given and know you've been blessed. And you'll hold it even tighter because you know you could lose it."

As she had lost her daughter...

"How did you keep going?" Garth asked, his voice a strangled whisper.

Nan reached over to squeeze his hand. "I had you."

The last bit of resistance melted away. If Nan could keep going in the face of such pain, how could he be too scared to even try? Garth slumped in his chair. "It's too late."

"Nonsense," Nan said crisply. "I don't know what you did to Melissa, but it's plain you messed up and you're going to make it right. It's going to be hard and scary but you're going to do it. Because the risk of losing her isn't worth the pain of knowing you didn't even try to hold on to her."

He paused, considering her words, knowing they were true. A single conclusion rang in his mind, excruciating in its simplicity.

He would have to win her back.

It wouldn't be easy. He hurt her and made her think she wasn't worth it. But she was, and every fiber of his being knew it was true. Now, he'd have to make sure she knew it, too.

Chapter Twenty-four

Melissa stared into her microwave, watching the frozen square of lasagna spin slowly on the glass plate. The thought of eating it made her gag. Maybe she'd just forget about it and have another pint of ice cream instead. That, and a few more aspirin.

Or maybe just a glass of wine.

She glanced at the clock. Just past noon. Maybe she'd wait a few hours before she opened the wine.

It was Saturday. The fourth day—not that she was counting—since she'd told him good-bye. No one knew what had happened. She'd told her co-workers at Solen Labs that she was sick and needed to work from home, even as she began to tie up some of her projects. She'd conferenced in for a few meetings. Garth, she noted, was absent from all of them, even the ones he had planned to attend.

"Where's the boss?" her friend Hal had asked her yesterday, in a staff meeting she'd attended by phone. "Is he sick, too?"

"You know him," she'd said with a laugh, making light of the question. "Never around when you need him." But the wondering about him never ceased. Was he avoiding her out of basic courtesy, or did he share some of this heart-wrenching pain? Had he already moved on, forgotten about the ring that she hadn't been able to remove from her finger? Did he regret pushing her away, or had he found a way to bury the emotion, like all the other feelings he'd squelched along the way?

The front door buzzed. Melissa glanced at her watch. Tori had said she might stop by, but she was supposed to be looking at office spaces for her new law practice until one.

Melissa pushed the intercom. "Yes?"

"'Lis, it's Brit. Can you come down for a minute? I need to show you something."

Though she knew it had to have been hard for him, Brit had been remarkably restrained since the night of the auction. He hadn't left for Aruba, like she'd suggested, but he hadn't made any new, dramatic, "I'll kill him" sort of pledges. No worried hovering or nagging. Just a quiet, concerned voice on the phone each morning. *Do you need anything? Can I come by tonight?*

What would he do when he found out the truth? That the engagement was over, and Garth wanted nothing to do with her? She dreaded that moment almost as much as she dreaded the prospect of waking up each morning without Garth's arms around her, or his lean body pressed against her side.

Melissa frowned. "Why don't you come up?"

"I can't. Just come down."

He sounded odd. Happy or sad, she couldn't tell. "What's going on?"

"'Lis." He put on his big brother voice. "Come down."

"Fine." She fluffed her bangs and grabbed her keys, waving at a neighbor as she made her way down the steps. When she pushed open the door her mouth fell open. "What the…" She sucked in a breath. "Garth? Mom? Tori?...Jess?!"

A small crowd had gathered around her stoop. Garth stood in the middle at the bottom of the steps. He held a small bouquet of pink roses in his hands. Just the sight of him—tall and broad-shouldered, his granite eyes fierce and strong—made her quiver, even while she told herself not to react to his presence.

He's done with you, remember?

To one side of Garth stood Nan, beaming happily. Jess stood at Nan's arm, pink tips of her hair gleaming. On the other side of Garth were Phoebe, John, Brit, and Tori. Ross and Joe were behind them. Ross's kids—Luke, Matt, and Julia—clustered around him. Felicity held Delia in her arms. Tori's eyes were suspiciously bright.

"I don't understand." Melissa stood still, blinking rapidly. "Garth, what's going on?"

She had a terrible, sinking feeling in her chest. Nan must have had a relapse, or something had gone wrong at work. This had to be an act Garth was putting on for someone's benefit. But why had he assembled her family? Why was Jess here? And if Nan was so sick, why did she look so relaxed and proud?

A stranger stepped forward. He was small and stout, and wore a short-sleeved, plaid oxford shirt and khaki pants held high on his stomach with a thick belt. In one hand, he held a notebook, which he flipped open. "Ms. Bencher," he said, "I'm Stanley Hartwaddle."

"What?" Melissa forced her gaze away from Garth, who was staring at her with an uncanny intensity. "Who?"

"Stanley Hartwaddle. I write for the *New York Star Herald*."

"Oh!" Melissa vaguely recalled his name attached to some articles about her and Garth. "Um, what the heck are you doing here?"

"Your fiancé asked me to come down and help."

"Help?" Melissa looked back at Garth, and then around the circle of grinning faces. Amid her confusion, a tiny shred of hope began to blossom in her chest.

"Yes, help." Stanley looked down at his notebook. "Mr. Solen has asked me to be the master of ceremonies for this event."

"This event?" Melissa cocked her head in confusion. "What event? Why isn't Garth speaking for himself? And why would he call in the press? You'll forgive me, but he hates the press."

"Apparently, that's part of the reason I'm here. He'd like for you to understand that he is willing to make this public in any forum you choose."

Melissa darted a look at Garth, and then glanced around the circle. "I'm not sure I have any idea what's going on, but okay. Go ahead."

Stanley cleared his throat. His carriage reminded Melissa of a medieval page, reading an important announcement from a scroll. "Mr. Solen has drafted a letter, which he will read in a moment. However, in light of his concern that he may lose his voice, or experience some emotional calamity which may make it difficult to speak, he has asked me to stand by and be prepared to step in as needed."

"Okay," Melissa said slowly. She stared at Garth, but directed her words to Stanley. "Why don't you tell him to go ahead."

Stanley nodded. "Mr. Solen," he said, with a regal gesture toward Garth. "I believe you may start."

Garth, who had been standing in uncharacteristic stillness, clutching the roses in his hand, stepped forward. He took a piece of paper from his pocket and unfolded it. He cleared his throat, and began to read.

"'My dearest Melissa, you know I am not good with words, particularly in a situation like this. One in which my very heart, my life, is on the line. So I've asked our friends and family to help me.'"

Melissa froze. Garth's gaze flickered from the paper to her face. She could feel the emotion spilling out from him in an intensity that transcended the physical distance between them.

"'I hope you don't mind that they are here, or that I have prepared this letter ahead of time. You know me well enough to understand how difficult this is, and how much it scares me to say these words. But in the past three weeks you have changed me. I thought I was destined for a life of solitude and loneliness. You made me realize I could have more. When you told me you loved me, I panicked. I thought it would be better to lose my chance at happiness than to risk losing my heart. But I was wrong.'"

Melissa fought a wave of tears. She raised one hand to her mouth as her chin trembled.

"'I love you, Melissa. I love you with every beat of my heart and breath in my lungs.'"

Garth paused and took a deep breath. He lowered the paper, and Melissa felt him caress her with the sweep of his gaze. When he spoke again, it was as if no one else was present, and he was speaking right into her heart. "You must know how sorry I am that I was too scared to say this before. I'm sorry that I did not know how to make sense of the feelings in my heart. I am even more sorry for any hurt I may have caused you. Nothing matters to me now but you, and my hope that you might be willing to give me a second chance."

Garth stopped. Stanley gestured toward John and Phoebe. "Mr. and Mrs. Bencher, I believe you are next."

Melissa brushed aside the tears spilling down her cheeks and turned to her parents.

"This morning, Garth called us," Phoebe said, smiling at Melissa. "He explained everything that had happened, and apologized for not coming to us sooner. Then he asked John for permission to marry you. For real."

Melissa gave a shaky laugh. "And?"

"I said yes." John looked back at Garth. "I admit I was skeptical, but this guy is truly in love with you. It didn't take much for us to change our minds."

"We hope you'll give him a second chance, Melissa," Phoebe said.

Stanley gestured toward Ross and Joe.

"Garth called us right after he spoke to Dad," Joe said, pushing his untidy hair out of his face and straightening his glasses. "He apologized for lying, and told us how he needed our support."

Ross gave Garth a meaningful look. "I told him he had a second chance, but not to count on a third."

Melissa gave a watery laugh. "Thanks, caveman."

Ross and Joe moved back and Tori and Brit approached Melissa. By this time, a small crowd of bystanders had begun to form. Garth didn't seem to notice, or care. He was focused on her, flowers still tightly gripped in one hand, eyes never straying from her face.

"Melissa, when I introduced you to Garth, I have to admit I had dreamed that maybe, possibly, you might be the one to bring him out of his shell." Tori beamed through her tears. "I really, really hope you give him another chance, because I can't imagine anyone I'd rather have for a sister."

Brit scowled, but Melissa saw a smile lurking in his eyes. "I told him he's the luckiest guy on earth," he said. "I also told him next time I'll give him a nose to match mine."

"My turn!" Nan chirped from the other side of the circle. "Melissa, dear, I can only tell you this: my grandson is far from perfect, but he's going to love you more than you can imagine. You'll have to help him sometimes, because he's going to do stupid things, but I promise, it will be worth it."

Jess nodded. "Yeah. What she said. He's not really a jerk. He just acts like one sometimes."

Everyone laughed, even the bystanders. When the sound had died down, Stanley waved at Melissa to get her attention. "Now, one last thing. Mr. Solen, if you please."

Garth came closer, stopping just a foot from the edge of the steps. "Melissa, I…" His voice cracked, and his lips twisted in a sheepish half smile. "Look, you know I'm miserable at this, but I…" He tried to say something else, but his voice caught in his throat.

Then he bent down on one knee and held out the roses. There was a pause as he struggled to find his voice, and Melissa had to restrain herself from hurtling her body down the steps at him. Finally, he looked back up at her. His granite eyes were soft, misty, and heartbreakingly hopeful. "Melissa Bencher, I love you with all my heart and soul. You're the part of me I didn't know was missing and the part I can't live without. You've already got my ring, twice over, but you've got my heart, too, and I can't imagine living without it, or you. Melissa, darling, will you marry me?"

"Yes, you silly man, yes! Yes!" Melissa flew down the steps, barely hearing the applause from the crowd. Garth stood as she reached him and swept her into his arms as she grabbed his shoulders. He hugged her around the waist, lifting her off the ground. His lips found hers in one long, perfect kiss. When he sat her back down, Melissa felt the love connecting and tying them together.

"Forever, my love," she whispered, holding his face in her

hands and kissing him one more time.

The circle of friends and family closed in around them. Her parents and brothers slapped Garth on the back, while Tori managed to wedge herself in between them for a double hug.

As the people crowded around, Melissa heard Stanley say to someone, "Now that's what I call a happy ending."

And it was.

Epilogue

"That is disgusting."

Melissa giggled at the look of horror on Luke's face. Ross's ten-year-old son might be comfortable putting spiders and toads into his pocket, but baby spit-up was completely outside his comfort zone.

"Honey, it's just a little bit of milk." She shifted the ruddy-cheeked baby on her chest and rubbed her cheek gently against his soft head. The smell of talcum powder, milk, and the indefinable scent of *baby* sent an avalanche of love over her.

"But it's, like, *chunky*." Luke recoiled further as Melissa wiped the white material from the infant's mouth with a soft cloth.

"Just imagine how much grosser the stuff that comes out the other end is." Ross sauntered across the room, grabbing Patrick from Melissa's arms without pause and moving to the window overlooking the backyard where Delia and Matt played on the newly appointed play structure. As he walked, Ross bounced the six-week-old with the ease of a three-time father.

It was Thanksgiving, and the entire Bencher family had joined Nan, Jess, Melissa, and Garth at Seesaw for the holiday. Even Brit and Tori had driven down for the night, though they planned to stay at a hotel a few miles away so Patrick wouldn't keep everyone awake at night. Nan sat in her favorite chair by the fire, watching the bustle of the family with a happy smile. Joe and Felicity had run into town to buy a can of cranberries, while Jess and Phoebe argued in the kitchen about how often to baste the turkey.

Melissa wasn't sure it was possible to be happier or more content. Even the house seemed to be glowing with the pleasure of full beds, a hot fire, and the noise of children running up and down the stairs.

"Where's Tori?" Ross asked.

"Grabbing a few minutes of sleep," Brit replied from the couch. "I think Paddy was up every hour last night." He set down the newspaper he'd been reading, stretched, and rubbed the thick dark shadow on his jaw. "And watch his head, would you? I'm not sure that's a good position for him. Who said you could hold him, anyway?"

Ross chuckled. "You're the worst new dad I've ever seen. I raised three of them, you know."

"Dad," Luke hollered from the back door, "Dad, I've got the football. You coming?"

"In a minute," Ross called.

Melissa joined her brothers at the window, watching as Luke ran outside, his breath making a frosty halo in the wintery air. "Did you tell them?" she asked.

Ross sighed. "No sense worrying them. Their mother just put her name in for the job in Colorado. It could be months before she hears anything."

Brit frowned. He reached out and took his son, easily shifting him over one shoulder. "And if she goes?"

Ross shrugged. "Then I go, too. I'm not having my kids halfway across the country from me."

"I know it's selfish, but I really hope she doesn't get the job." Melissa sighed and leaned against the window. Though the thought of her brother leaving was painful, it wasn't a surprise. Ross was willing to do just about anything for his kids—even if that meant dropping everything to be with them.

At the sound of her voice, Brit turned, eyes narrowed. "You okay, 'Lis? You're looking a little pale."

She cleared her throat. "I'm fine." A wave of nausea threatened her casual dismissal of his concern, but she fought it off. "Just tired. Garth and I have been working late all week, trying to get the data from the ThinkSpeak prototypes analyzed before the holiday. We should be ready to get our first two commercial units in the field by Christmas."

Brit glowered. "If you're getting sick, you better stay away from Patrick."

Ross eyed her shrewdly. "Wait a minute, are you—"

He was interrupted by the arrival of Garth, carrying a steaming cup of peppermint tea. Even though they'd been married for almost six months, the sight of Garth's tall, broad-shouldered form still had the power to make Melissa quiver, especially when he gave her that look—the one that wrapped her in a cocoon of love and concern.

"Can I get you anything else?" he asked, passing her the mug as he dropped a kiss on her cheek. Warm gray eyes gazed deep into hers as he wrapped a protective arm around her waist. "Crackers, maybe?"

A tiny smile began to dance in the corner of Ross's mouth. "Crackers and peppermint tea, huh?"

Garth turned to Ross, his face a polite mask. "You have a problem with crackers and tea?"

Ross's smile broadened. "Don't even try that ice man thing on me, brother. I know you too well for that."

Brit's gaze moved back and forth between them. "Wait, what am I missing?"

"Sleep deprived much?" Ross said with a laugh. "Look at them! Garth's all lit up like a—well, like you. Like a worried father."

"Worried—" Brit drew in a breath. "Father? Jesus, Melissa, why didn't you tell us?" He grabbed her in an unceremonious hug, almost sending her tea sailing through the air.

Melissa tried to bury her guilty smile. She shushed and pushed him off, darting a look at Nan, who had just nodded off in her chair. "We haven't even seen a doctor yet. And we want to wait until we're further along before we tell Nan. Just in case."

Ross nodded. "I understand." He claimed his own bear hug from Melissa, and then clasped Garth's hand and shook it heartily. "Congratulations. I'm thrilled for you."

Garth's attempt at stoicism fell away. His shoulders dropped and he shook his head in wonder. He gathered Melissa into his arms, spooning her back against his stomach and dropping his head into the curve of her neck. "Thanks. But I have no idea how you guys survived this. I'm a wreck and it's only been two weeks. How the hell are we going to get through nine months?"

Brit grinned. "Oh, you'll make it."

Ross nodded. "You'll be fine. You've got each other."

Melissa tipped her head to the side and looked at Garth. He whispered in her ear. "If you'll still have me?"

She sighed happily. "Forever, my love. Forever."

About the Author

Inara Scott grew up on a steady diet of romance and happily ever after. Her first novel, penned at the age of 14, was titled *A Wild and Stormy Passion* and featured a sword-wielding pirate heroine. Today, Inara writes anything and everything, including young adult fiction and adult romance. Rumors of her secret life as a university professor, writing about energy law and economics, also circulate. She does frequent school visits and enjoys teaching writing to students of all ages. Inara loves to hear from readers. You can contact her via her website, at www.inarascott.com, or find her on Facebook (www.facebook.com/inarawrites) or on Twitter (@inarascott).

Made in the USA
San Bernardino, CA
13 March 2017